SHE'LL TAKE YOUR WORLD

Kim McCall
aka/Travel

She'll Take Your World

ACKNOWLEDGMENTS

I want to give God glory for helping me with this novel. I also want to acknowledge my daughter Ms. Nataya B., my son Mr. Jamar C. dba www.Gametimeacademy.org, my grandson Isaiah C. and his mother Ms. Maria A. Maria has always supported me in everything I've done, My mother Sandra N., my dad that raised me, Mr. Charles Scrogging II and my father that birthed me, Mr. Charles Perkins. After 37 years of looking for my long-lost siblings, I'm happy to have met Ms. Shelly B. of Minneapolis, MN, Mrs. Alice F. of Melbourne, FL, and Mr. David P. Eugene. Thank you to my editor Ms. Nika Michelle, my proofreaders Mrs. Mary, Burt B. and Walter Banks Jr., as well as Ms. Meredith M. for reading and letting me use her voice for my audio book that is coming soon. Thank you, Aunt Stephany P., my best friend Mr. CJ, the pilot who gave me all the correct information on airport terms, and Mr. Vincent Burrell who invested in my first novel. To my brother from another mother, Mr. Edward Osborne, Ms. Tammy Capri, who created my fabulous cover for my novel, and Mr. Don M., who helped with my web site, thank you. Thank you to my best friend in Minneapolis. MN and Mr. Music for all the good feedback. To all my family, fans and colleague who pushed me to finish this novel, I couldn't thank you enough.

DEDICATION

*This novel is dedicated to all the married couples,
people who are thinking about getting married and people
who are in a relationship.*

To contact Ms. Kim, go to
www.iammskim.com

TABLE OF CONTENTS

BKH

(Basically Known as a Hoe)

What's up y'all? My name is Reginae Arnold, but my nickname is Nae-Nae. Some of my family and friends call me *Pretty Chocolate*. Yeah, it's cute. My first boyfriend, Walter Green, gifted me with it. Let's be clear, I only let my close friends call me *Pretty Chocolate*. It just stuck. I am known as a "pretty little chocolate girl." Before we get into all that, let me tell you a little bit about my family. My mama was never home, because she was out doing her own thing in the streets, coming home in the wee hours of the morning. My daddy was a hustler who made his money shooting dice and playing cards. My life was void of any good influences, so I had to teach myself all about morals and values. The only lessons that I learned from both of my parents were, a lazy hustler did not get bread nor fed, and being broke and hungry is *not* cute! Mama told me that I could have almost any man I wanted. That was right before she said that they would "pay my bills, give me good lovin' and money to blow." Sooo, if I follow her wondrous advice, I will never be without? Hmmm…let me marinate on that for a minute. Growing up the child of two hustlers, the house was always filled with interesting, but weird characters who showed up late at night. There were times when they'd be so loud and belligerent, and cursing like I wasn't even there. That was how I learned so many forbidden words. Fights had even broken out a few times right in front of me. Sometimes, I would come home to find people asleep in my bed. It was all a bit much for a young girl. No one told me, what my mama did for living until I got older. Once the truth came out, it changed my life forever.

During my childhood, I felt alone. It was mostly just me, myself and I. My mama and daddy were almost never home. Being an only child, my first cousin (and my best friend) Portia, was my *only* friend. Some would say that I raised myself. It wasn't unusual at all for me to get up at 5:00 a.m. to prepare for school all alone. One early winter morning, I decided to cut class to look for a job. Being that my mama and daddy are not reliable, I could really use the money. Living with them was something I really hated with a passion! In the spring, I will be graduating from high school in just a few more months after, I'll be off to college. A girl has got to step up her game if I wanted to get away from my unfit parents and their company. There is no way I can be dropping out of school for being a teenage mom. That is not an option! Usually if I can't sleep, I'll just lay in bed thinking and counting imaginary $100 bills. There is so much on my mind tonight…I just can't sleep. Maybe a bath will do. In the process of planning my day it occurred to me that the only way I'm going to get out of this hell hole is to dig my way out! I'm in desperate need of a job ASAP and so I had to do what I had to do!

Suddenly, my cell phone rings. It is about six in the morning and I wonder who could

be calling me this early? Who died? By the ringtone, I instantly know it is Portia. Her favorite song is Beyonce's "Sorry", so it was only right that I set it as her ringtone.

"Whew! Nae-Nae, girl I'm rolling today!" Her voice was loud and filled with excitement.

"What you rolling? A blunt? Some burritos?"

"You got jokes trick! No, I got my mom's car and I was calling to see if you need a ride to school? She's out of town visiting her sister, so I got you boo!"

Her goody two shoe butt was going to school and she had her mother's whip. I'd be playing hooky. "Girl, my head is killin' me. Can you get my homework from Mr. Smith's class?"

"Lord, did you take your blood pressure pills? You need to take your pills girl. I need you here forever and you know we got a test on Friday?"

Wanting to reach right through the phone and give her a hug, I couldn't help but think about how she is always looking out for me. "Portia, what would I do without you? Now get yo' butt to school."

"A'ight cuz! I'll hit you up later."

We hang up and I decide to go ahead and take advantage of that hot, bubble bath. Maybe then I'll be able get my mind right The water feels so good as I lower my body into the hot, fragrant bubbles. I had used my own money to take advantage of a sale at Bath and Body Works. Japanese Cherry Blossom is my favorite fragrance and so I had the entire set. In no time, I am feeling more relaxed than before. After realizing that my finger tips and toes are wrinkled I decide to get on out.

Once I am out of the bathtub, I lay across the bed, thinking of what I can do to move out of this house and get my own apartment. Hmmm…there has to be a solid plan A, B, and C, for me to see my way out. If nothing else, mama taught me that. That's when I jump up out of the bed, went to my computer and start to look for jobs online. A job in the medical field would be ideal, but I am not exactly sure what I want to do. That's when my eyes focus on a particular posting: *No experience needed; will train the right candidate. Need a Front Desk Receptionist ASAP. Please call the number below after you have submitted your application to set up an interview.* There must be a god, because I need *that* job more than I needed to breath! To be honest, I needed that job like two years ago! It is like everything is a blur as I notice that it is 7:00 a.m. Let me go ahead fill out this application, really quick! I'm feeling a little nervous. Well, I am feeling a lot nervous. What will I say? But, I really need to call, NOW! Sending up a little prayer, I pick up the phone and proceed to dial the number. The deep, baritone voice of a man tantalizes my ears. Dang, he sounded super sexy.

"Dr. Rocky Lift's office. Who do I have the pleasure of speaking with today?"

Starting to say *Pretty Chocolate*, I catch myself.

"My name is Reginae Arnold. I just submitted my application for the Receptionist position that I saw the ad for online. Can you transfer me to Human Resources?"

"Yes, I can assist you with that. I am Human Resources, Accounts Payable…you name it!" He chuckles.

"Oh, okay! Has the position been filled?

"No, but you may be in luck! Could you come in for an interview today? Looking at Dr. Lift's schedule, 3 p.m. works best for him. Will that work for you?"

"Yes, I'll be there. I just need the address."

He proceeds to give me directions to an address located in the luxurious Beverly Hills. Beverly Hills? What in the world have I stumbled upon? I'm about to get that *big* money. Shoot, I am about to be moving on up! The thought makes me look this Dr. Rocky Lift up. Not wanting to get my hopes up for nothing, it is a must for me to make sure he is legit. Whoa, I am instantly impressed after my Google search! This doctor is one of the top board-certified plastic surgeons in California. For a young chick, I'm creepin' on a come-up! God is good! My prayers are finally being answered! First thing's first though. Needing to borrow a car stopped me in my tracks. That's when I decide to go see my cousin Squirrel who he lives next door with his father, my Uncle Frank. Squirrel always sleeps during the day and kicks it in the streets at night. No one really knows what he does for a living, but Squirrel always keeps a large amount of cash in his pocket. It didn't take a rocket scientist to figure out the fact that he got his money illegally. You can say he's a big baller, and shot caller on the west coast. After I knock all hard on the door, I wait for him to answer. Slowly, he opens the screen door.

"What you want Nae-Nae?"

"Let me borrow your car, cuzzo! Mine is in the shop. It needs a tune-up."

"It's all good yo'. When you get back come on in through the back door. I'm gon' leave it unlocked. Just put the keys on the counter. Of course, make sure you lock up, too! Don't need my stuff stolen. You know how these greedy fools are out here. They think you got something, they gon' try and take it. You feel me?" His stone-cold eyes bore into mine as I nod in agreement.

"I got you cuzzo...I'll be back in a few!"

Once I have my transportation situation handled, I start dressing in a frenzy. It isn't like my wardrobe is spectacular, so it took me a while to put something decent together. Deciding on a navy-blue pencil skirt and white blouse, I slide my feet into a pair of old, worn out black heels. In no time, it's almost 2 p.m. and I'm nowhere near ready. All I have to do is put a little makeup on and brush my hair. Am I crazy? I've always wanted to trade my body in for a better one. You know, like the girl who never gets a muffin top, or love handles, even after stuffing down a double bacon cheeseburger, fries and extra-large root beer. You know what I'm talking about; that coke bottle figure. Working out two times a week at the gym has its rewards, but I'm not seeing any yet. One day, I'm going to upgrade to a more expensive health club. That can be handled later…I've got an interview to get too! Walking over to Uncle Frank's house, I hurried toward the back door, went inside, grabbed the keys off the counter and locked up. Squirrel had a nice, black, 2017 BMW convertible. After admiring the leather seats, I started the engine, drove away from the curb and on to my interview.

The weather is real crisp and cool, but has cleared up of the rain from the previous day. Wanting to drop the top and show off, I couldn't because it was too cold. Besides, even if it was warm, it took too long for me to get this hair on fleek! Not that familiar with this area in Beverly Hills, I rely on my GPS to get me there quickly and away from traffic! The GPS tells me that I am twenty-two minutes away from my destination. That isn't too bad at all, because I am making good time. When I pull up into the parking lot, I am indeed shocked. Wow! This neighborhood looks like a scene out of one of those reality shows. As I get out of the car and walk towards the building, I spot two movie stars and one fine rapper coming out of the building. My eyes light up like NY's Times Square on Christmas. When I get this job, I'll be rolling in money! I look the part. I *am* the part. My hair and outfit are fleekish and my confidence is at an all-time high! *I want this job! I claim it! I believe it. I will receive it!* Mama taught me to say that if I ever wanted *something*. Right at that moment, I realize that I hadn't wanted anything in my life more.

There is no one sitting at the receptionist desk. The phone rings about fifty-eleven times and that makes me think about the job at hand. Was the phone always that lit? A small bell is sitting there, so I tap it about three times. Duh! You're supposed to ring the bell. There are two men and three women sitting down in the waiting area. One of the men is listening to music with some earbuds, the other man is texting, and the three ladies are reading from their handheld tablets. As I glance towards the fish tank that sits nestled in the corner near the bathroom, I see this fine man walk up to me. He is at least 6'1 with pretty hazel brown eyes, long, black dreadlocks and a beard groomed to perfection. Inadvertently, I begin licking my lips lustfully. He looks mmm, mmm, good and it's as if my reaction is beyond my control! If only you could see those lips of his for yourself. They are so full, with the perfect brown tone. This guy is hot as fish grease and I can't help but stare. It is obvious that he is a doctor, being that he has on a white lab coat. Before I have the chance to speak, he does.

"Hello! You must be Reginae Arnold."

Clearing my throat, I manage to get out a simple, "Yes."

"My name is Dr. Rocky Lift. I've reviewed your resume, which is very impressive for a high school student. You are a high school student, correct?"

"Yes, Dr. Lift! I'll be graduating soon and headed to college."

"By the way, you look...fantastic." Dr. Lift is acting kind of thirsty. He just doesn't know, but I can be the one to quench that thirst! There is no way I can't keep checking him out. You know how we do ladies. We start from the feet and work our way up! My cheeks are beginning to hurt from smiling. He even has pretty, straight, white teeth, which is not surprising to me at all. Dr. Lift motions to one of his patients, by lifting one finger, letting him know that he will be with him shortly. A medical assistant walks out from the back in baby blue scrubs.

"Should I put Bruce in exam room number one, Dr. Lift?"

"Yes," he nods his agreement in her direction, but keeps his sexy eyes trained on me.

"My apologies. I have to still keep things going. Where were we?"

This gorgeous guy is polite, too. That is my kind of man. "You told *me* that I looked fantastic. Thank you!"

"You're very welcome! Now, this is a part-time position. Only twenty guaranteed hours, four days a week. You're still in high school, so it's important to keep a good GPA."

"It's cool, Dr. Lift!" What am I doing? There's no need to get too casual with him. He's

still the boss! "You caught me off guard, Dr. Lift. Sorry. You're right. I am keeping my GPA up." Truth be told, my eye is on another job. Whoever gives me the most coins, gets *me*!

"So, have you decided what field of study you'd like to go into?" Those deep eyes of his were still glued to mine.

"Yes, Dr. Lift. I want to become a doctor." It was like I had to look away from him to focus on my thoughts. Suddenly, Dr. Lift was making me want this job more regardless of the pay. Seeing his sexy self every day was incentive enough. Then I scratched that thought, I had to be all about my paper.

"Very impressive. Medicine is a very rewarding field. The result is you'll change people's lives and make a great living. What college will you be attending in the fall?"

"Somewhere, here in California. I haven't decided yet."

A large, infectious smile spread across lips, revealing deep dimples. That smile says,

'Take your clothes off!' I want to reply, "Any day!" The phone begins to ring more and more. The stress on Dr. Lift's face begins to show clearly.

"I've interviewed over ten people today," he starts and then, he immediately changes the

subject. Checking him out again, I gaze into his eyes and then let mine linger on his juicy lips. This man is way too fine! The thing is, I am not eighteen yet, so I am not legal. Dr. Lift is still talking, but I am off in la-la land. By the time, my eyes drift down to his crotch, it is time for a well-needed pause. He's packing a monster!' My mind drifts, wondering how big and long it is?

"Reginae, are you okay?"

Hearing him say my name makes me snap back into reality, killing the freaky fantasy that crept into my mind. "Yes," slips out in a whisper as I continue to look at him in awe.

Look at those big hands…and he smells sooo good. Never have I seen a man so well put together. His pecs and biceps are protruding through his white lab coat. I love a man over 6'1 and he had to be at least 6'3! My temperature is rising and my panties are getting extra moist to the point of sticking to my flesh. If only he knew. My body is working overtime and there is nothing I can do to stop it!

"Let me know if you need any references for college. My connections are abundant. I could help you get anywhere in the medical field. I have several professors who are close friends of mine. One of them may be able to assist you with choosing a school as well as your course load."

"Well, four colleges have offered me a full ride. I just need to pick one. As soon as I make a choice, I'll let you know." He seems really relaxed with me and we both are obviously enjoying each other's conversation. Dr. Lift looks super young, but he's making good paper! He must be way older than I am, being that it takes years of medical school to become a doctor with your own practice. Wondering how much he's going to pay me, I decide to ask.

"How much will I be paid per hour, Dr. Lift?"

"Let's start you out with twelve dollars an hour and go from there."

That made me almost crap in my pants. All I was expecting was minimum wage. He must be doing very well. The little experience I had, I decided to share with him. Dr. Lift needs to know. Shoot, he might pay me more!

"I'm very efficient in 10-key by touch, and average about 10,000 keystrokes per minute. If you need a letter, or any document, I can type 55 words per minute."

He smiled that sexy smile of his and I could tell that he was very impressed. The phones kept ringing off-the-hook. Dr. Lift had to stop the interview twice to answer it. After the last call, he picked up the phone, placed the caller on hold and turned to look at me.

"Are you really interested in this position, Reginae?

"Yes, sir!" I can start *now…on* him!

"Great! When can you start? "

"I can come back tomorrow…"

Cutting me off, he asks, wearing a desperate expression, "How about now?"

A puzzled look is on my face. Is this man for real?

"Why not? Let me see how proficient you are. You'll get off at 5 p.m."

Without a second thought, I agree. "Sure! Uh, I just need to make a personal call soon."

"Not a problem at all."

The phone blared and he gave me a stern look as if he wanted to play boss. It was okay, being that it turned me on.

That's when I sat down and began answering calls and making appointments. As Dr. Lift is walking away, he informs me that a nurse will relieve me in about ten minutes. Well, ten minutes passed pretty quickly and a nurse walks up to the front desk. She introduces herself briefly as the head nurse. "There are five nurses and one medical assistant who work in this office. You will get to meet each of them later. This office is a hot mess honey." Right away, the nurse started giving me all the 411 on the office. She told me that Dr. Lift's wife and sister-in-law had got mad at each other two days ago and came up in the office causing all types of drama with the staff. Apparently, things got so heated that some of staff walked off the job. Mrs. Lift even gave her husband the finger and told him to stick it where the sun didn't shine. "Lordt," what in the world? According to her, it was always some drama with his wife because she was a bourgeois, stuck up chick with a big mouth.

"I have so much more to share, but we'll talk later. Go make your call. I'll cover the front desk for you."

Stepping outside to call my cousin Squirrel, I let him know that I will be home around 5:30 p.m. He let me know that he had just woke up anyway. Then he offers to drop me off at the shop to pick up my whip. How nice of him. Wait. What did he want? It was as if I could see the big smile on his face just by hearing his voice.

"Cuzzo, I got me a job! Now, I'm gon' be makin' paper like you!"

"Nae-Nae, you lyin! Where? McDonalds?"

"You know you clowning, fool! In Beverly Hills! Yeah, you heard that right! Now what? Put some respect on my name!"

His voice changed, because I shocked the hell out of him. By now he's laughing at me.

"Are you for real, cuzzo? You so ratchet... Who's the new cutty buddy?" He actually thinks I gave up some cut to get a job. Nah! Never! In that case, I didn't need a job. I'd just get a cutty buddy with some cash and milk him. That would've been so much easier anyway.

"Mind your business...you'll live longer. Boy, bye!"

With that said, I hung up in his face, walked back into the office, thanked the head nurse for covering the phone, and sat back down. She insisted that I help her with getting the patients in and out.

"It's the the only way to go home on time," she added for good measure.

Dr. Lift's staff was on top of their game at closing time and made sure the last patient was seen by 4:30 p.m. The head nurse walked around the pod demanding that all PCs be shut down by 4:55 p.m. One lady even bragged that she had a hot date with a wealthy attorney and she must be out by 5 p.m. Wow! The nerve of these people. You really don't go home until the work is done! Trying to make conversation with her and the other employees, I commented on how bad traffic was in California. Everybody agreed.

"They don't know it, but I'm not eating dinner at 10 p.m. That's a lie", I scoffed.

When I started to walk out the door with everybody else, Dr. Lift called my name.

"Reginae, could you step into my office for a few minutes. I won't keep you very long," he pleaded.

That's when I put on my cute voice. "Sure, doctor. I'm on my way!"

Everybody says their goodbyes and applaud me on a job well done. I wonder what he wants. Walking back to Dr. Lift's office, I look around his office, admiring his degrees on the wall. He is really a big time plastic surgeon with all types of plaques! He even has a humongous fish tank built into the floor. Now, that is dope! As I look over to my left, I notice that his office is connected to an apartment. The door is wide open. There is a beautiful shower made of glass. That is fire! Then, I notice that to my right, there is a beautiful view of a lake. It all looks just like a scene out of a movie. How do people make enough money to live like this? One day, I'm going to have just as much as he has, if not more!

"I asked you back to my office to thank you for pitching in and being a team player. My head nurse told me you did a great job. Are you coming back tomorrow?"

"Yes, sir! I'll be here." In that moment, I am mesmerized by all my good fortune. All of a sudden, his cell phone rings. Dr. Lift excuses himself to another room. His anger is apparent with the caller. In between expletives, mentions of his wife and sister-in-law and him kicking the wall, he begins to shout louder and louder. "If my wife thinks she's going to get my money, she's got another thing coming!" And with that, he puts the caller on hold.

"I'm so sorry Reginae... but I have to take this call. It's my brother Dr. Keoni calling from Seattle. You have a good evening! See you tomorrow!"

"Goodbye," I respond and walk away.

As I am walking out, I can hear him talking about me. "Yeah man, I hired this nice, smart, young lady! Bro, she got a big ol' butt, but she's a senior in high school."

I told you he was thirsty. Anyway, I'm feeling him whether I'm in high school, or not! He has nice lips, firm abs and then some! He just doesn't know the things I could do to him. He is more mature than the boys at my school and he has lots of money. If he makes a move, I'll be all game. I will be eighteen soon, so age won't matter soon. After I jumped in the driver's seat of my cousin's car, I pulled off immediately. When I called Squirrel, he picked up on the second ring. The loud, pulsating beat of some trap music played in the background. Squirrel was always lit! The music he listens to gives a hint of his lifestyle. If it isn't about selling drugs, hoes and spending money, he isn't going to listen to it.

"What's up with you girl? You on your way? I got things to do! Big T wants me to meet him at seven. Grown man ish...you heard?"

"Squirrel, what kind of business you got goin' on? You know that with what you do, you don't have to be nowhere at a designated time."

"Look cuzzo, just get them four wheels 'round here. Bein' nosey. You know he asked about you yesterday. He want to know if you can come with us. I think he sweet on you, yo'. He want to make you his boo-thang." He laughs all loud and obnoxious.

If looks could kill, Squirrel would be dead. Letting out a snicker, I must shut him down. "I will not talk to that dude, so you know I will not be his boo! He makes me sick to my stomach. He's too old for all that gold in his mouth. Brushing his teeth won't help either. He needs veneers. Aha! There is one way to stop him from bugging me. Give him my government phone number that I never pick up!" These sorry men…

"You wrong for that Nae! That man loves you!"

"Bye, cuzzo! Get off my phone! I'll see you in a minute."

Traffic was heavy leaving the office, so I was at my cousin's house in forty minutes flat. Squirrel was standing outside smoking a Black and Mild. He motioned for me to pull up.

"Nae-Nae, you late yo'! I told you I had something to do! Dang!"

Rolling my eyes, I spat, "Better late than never, Squirrel! I'm here a'ight! Chill out!"

"Get over on the passenger side. I'm driving! I'll drop you off to get your car and then I'm going to meet up with Big T. I'll tell him you said, hi!"

That's when I raise my eyebrows in disgust. Squirrel starts laughing so hard that tears are rolling down his face. He drops me off, I thank him and throw up the deuces. Off we both go in opposite directions. It's so unbelievable that I got a job that easily. Maybe I could save up enough money to get my own apartment. It's this girl's dream to walk around my own crib in my birthday suit. I had never really been a fan of clothes, because they're so restrictive! In my opinion, it would be a perfect world if we all could walk around nude. The real world shuns that though, and I didn't want to end up locked up for indecent exposure. Not able to wait to tell my best friend Portia, my next thought is to call and share the news. She will be so happy for me!

As if on cue, my cell phone rings. By that unmistakable ringtone, I know it is Portia.

"Girl, I got a new job making bank in Beverly Hills!" As Drake's "Pop Style" plays on my Pandora station, I begin to mimic the beat, tapping on the steering wheel with my fists. It's seriously making me want to pull this car over and dance right now. "Twerk a lil' something! Ayeee!" If I knew that I could do it without some impatient person with road rage honking at me, I would.

"Who you cuttin' *Pretty Chocolate*?"

You hella wrong…I'm not cuttin' no one!"

"Can I borrow some coins, since you rich and all now. Maybe we can be roommates."

"Ha-ha-ha! Love you girl, but NO ma'am!"

It is clear in her voice that she is mad with me, but I don't care. By now, I can tell she wants to get off the phone with me. "I'll call you later then, since you all brand new now," she hisses with an attitude.

"Get all out yo' feelings. I was just playing" That didn't change the fact that I didn't want to be her roommate. "Hold up, girl! Did you get my homework from Mr. Smith?"

I got you girl! I'll wrap it up in a bow… like a present of sorts. Will that make you happy?"

"Whatever! Could you drop it off and put it in my mailbox? I'm not going home, because I need to stop at the store. Uh, we'll talk later. Holla boo!"

After talking to my big sis, all these different thoughts begin to flood my mental. Does Dr. Lift think I'm sexy? Well, I think I'm sexy…I'm going to treat myself to something that fits my voluptuous curves just right! What will mama and daddy think once I tell them I plan to move out? It doesn't matter at this point, being that I'm almost grown and can make my own decisions. There is just something about Dr. Lift that makes me feel sexy and I want to explore that.

The next couple of months were difficult, as I was cramming hard for my finals and working hard at Dr. Lift's office. Before the day of my 18th birthday, my hands began to shake a lot as I began packing my clothes for the move. What in the world? Am I that nervous? I was taught to be brave and express my feelings fully. Why am I second guessing myself? I decides to tell my daddy that I was moving when the time was right. When I wake up the next morning, it dawns on me that it's my 18th birthday!!! I'm thinking about wearing some short shorts and a cute crop top, since it's a hot, spring day.

Daddy woke up early that morning to start the barbeque and began setting up the backyard, as my Uncle Frank & cousin Squirrel helped. Although I'd invited all my coworkers, I am not sure if they will come through. You already know the fam and classmates were invited for sure! All in all, I had invited a total of 75 people, but only 50 RSVP'd. It's all good…It's their loss.

"It's my birthday! It's my birthday! Ayeee!" I can drink now! Should I have a glass of wine? Beer? Choices, choices, choices! At eighteen, a girl can really turn-up! There is a knock on my door. It is my mama telling me to get my butt out the bed. She wants me to come in the kitchen to read off my wish list.

After I go downstairs, I sit down at the breakfast bar. Mama passes me my list back and points to the check marks listed next to the items I requested. I am shocked, truly shocked…to see that mama got *everything* on my list. Does she think I don't know *what* she's doing? Mama always takes my money and does whatever. It comes on the 15th of each month. No one knows it, but I'm paying for my own party. That reality is not going to ruin my day. Deciding to relax in a hot bath before getting ready, I start fantasizing about the things I could do to Dr. Rocky Lift. Letting my mind wander, I imagine that I am sitting in a chair completely naked and relaxed, while soft music plays in the background. Candles are lit everywhere in my new apartment. The candles' scent, flood the room with the tropical aroma of a blend of oranges and pineapples. It feels like a scene right out of a romantic movie.

Everything is set up on one single chair, right in the middle of the living room. The picture I am painting in my mind has Dr. Lift knock on the door and I let him in after taking my time. Anticipation was key to make the night even more hot and steamy. He sees me sitting in the chair as he locks the door behind him. He begins to peel off his clothes gradually, dropping them behind him as he closes the short distance between us. The bathroom walls are all wet and steamed up as my breathing becomes labored. My head is leaning back in the chair, while he drops down on his knees in front of me. He starts to playfully nibble on one of my toes and then proceeds to lick from my calves to my inner thighs. Although I'm fantasizing, I'm worrying if I shaved my kitty last night. The thought makes me let out a giggle. The heat of his tongue causes my body to overcome with passion and unadulterated desire. By now, his face is deep up in my cookies enjoying the sweet taste of my goodies.

"Mmmm…" A moan actually escapes my lips. What a fantasy! If only it could really come true? If I played my cards just right, maybe it would. Besides, I was officially legal now. That would make my day, week, month and year! If only Dr. Lift was aware of the feelings I harbored for him? A knock is heard on my bathroom door and it's mama checking on me. She messed up my wet dream. It was time for me to get out anyways!

After lifting myself from the tub reluctantly, I turn on the ceiling fan to cool my feverish

flesh down. Once my hair is curled and done up, I apply my makeup and decide to wear some jean shorts with a crop top. Walking out of my bedroom, I lock the door behind me. The sound of male voices let me know that some dudes were laughing while playing cards and dominoes. The music was lit. All my favorite songs were playing, one after another. The party was supposed to start at 2 that afternoon. Most of my coworkers were already there by 2:15, including Dr. Rocky Lift. My family and friends did not show up until 3:15. They are always late for everything. Suddenly, my best friend Portia walks up to me.

"Those two guys want to dance with us," she tells me with a sly grin on her pretty

face. Then she grabs one of my arms. "Let's go dance with them. We don't have anything else to do!" As I stare down at my modest outfit, I begin to feel some type of way. I didn't have the best clothes and my shoes were outdated too! My mama and daddy have no clue that I hate living with them. The only reason I stayed this long was to save money to move. Real talk, mama and daddy didn't really care about me. All they want is my money. My high school is private and I have a scholarship to attend. Every month, I receive a small stipend for maintaining a 4.0 GPA. My parents would always brag about how they are proud me. How are you proud of me and still taking *my* money? So, now you know why I want to move OUT!

One of my earliest memories is watching my mama and daddy stuff money in their mattress. They'd cut a small hole in it and keep stuffing all their money inside. Back then, no one trusted banks. This influenced me to do the same. I'd even stuff coins in there. In my opinion, all money counts. Everyone walks up to me, pinning money to my shirt. They pin tens, twenties, fifties and even $100 bills. There is so much money the pin is too small to hold it all. Then, people start giving it to me in my hand. Both of my hands are full of money.

"Portia, hold the party down for me boo, while I handle my business." Opening a drawer in the kitchen, I grab a sharp knife, and wrap it up in a towel so that nobody can see it. After that, I hightailed it to my bedroom and locked the door. Once the hole is cut in my mattress, I start to count it. By the time I'm finished, I have $1,500.00. My eyes light up with dollar signs. Taking the rest of the money, I start shoving it inside my mattress.

Never had I had this much money in my life, ever! One day I will be making money like this. Today, on my 18th birthday, I declare that I will never ever, ever, ever be broke like my parents. The struggle is real! Trying to prepare breakfast with little to no choices to eat, like oatmeal and some wheat bread; no protein at all. Let's not even go into dinner! I had to eat canned beans, greens, tomatoes, potatoes. You name it! With this promising job at Dr. Lift's office, I know that brighter days are ahead. Portia knocked hard on the door.

"Slow poke, hurry up! We ready to sing and cut this cake!"

Immediately when I get to the backyard, my mama stops the music and asks everybody to sing happy birthday. This is the best day ever. My only wish is to get out of this hell hole of a home! After my mama cuts the cake, some of my family and friends stand around talking and dancing.

This good looking, old man keeps staring me down while licking his lips. That makes me feel very uncomfortable. A granddaddy is not on the agenda and neither is a sugar daddy! Just give me the money, honey! Turning my back on him, I stroll towards my cousin Squirrel and tells him that this old head was staring me down. To be honest, I'd had enough of that perv.

Somebody needs to put him on blast! Enough is enough!

"You don't know who that is?" Squirrel gestures as his hand covers his mouth.

"If I knew who he was, I would tell my mama." By now, I'm getting more & more pissed off. It's my birthday and I do not want anybody messing up my day.

Squirrel finally speaks up. "That's your mama's boss, Leroy."

"So, why the hell is he staring at me?" In frustration, I walk away from him and over to the table where Dr. Lift is sitting all by himself. That man has to know how fine he is! Smelling good, and looking like a bag of money. He makes me hot just by the mere sight of him. Casually touching his leg, I decide to test the waters. I begin to rub his leg this time and he never once attempts to move my hand. Is this my green light?

Dr. Lift's marriage doesn't mean anything to me. The way I felt, may the best woman win.

"Are you enjoying yourself? It's no Beverly Hills swag! I know that…"

"Nae-Nae, I'm enjoyin' myself." Yes, we have become close enough for him to call me that. "The music is the perfect blend of old and new school…love it!" he beams.

"Dr. Lift, I'm glad you're my boss. You're so down to earth

"We're not at work right now, so let your hair down! Call me Rocky." Then, he suddenly changes the subject. "Who cooked these ribs? This food is bomb!"

"Well, It's compliments of my daddy, the chef! Glad you like the food."

"Can I take you out for your birthday? My treat, for being such a good employee.

Beaming at him, I didn't hesitate. "Yes, Rocky!" Now, I'm smiling from ear to ear.

"My brother is coming into town next Friday from Seattle, so how about Saturday night? He begins to fidget with his watch, while staring dead into my eyes. Never taking him for the nervous type, I let out a soft giggle.

"Once you meet my brother, you'll love him. He's a doctor, like me. It'll be easier for me to pick you up and drop you off. Is that okay?" By now my heart is racing and I'm overwhelmed with excitement. Saturday couldn't come quick enough.

"Yes, can't wait to hit the town!"

Then he looks down at his cell phone. "I'm sorry, I have to take this." Rocky gets up and walks a few feet away to drown out the music. After he walks back to the table, he shares with me that he has a patient experiencing complications after her surgery. "I have to go now. She's having difficulty breathing. I told her to call 911 and I'll meet her at the hospital."

"Wow, you must go! It's important. I understand one hundred percent."

"I just performed her breast augmentation surgery a week ago. She went from an A-cup to a C -cup."

"I'm jealous. That's what I want for my 19th birthday."

He looks at me, flashes a big smile and waves goodbye. I hate to see him leave, but I love to watch him go. Damn, baby! That man is everything I've ever dreamed of in my life wrapped up in a fine, built package. His money was the bow to tie it all together perfectly. Mmm!

The party went off with a bang. Everybody enjoyed themselves, including me. There is a bottle of wine on the table calling my name. I know I'm not legally old enough to drink, but it's my birthday! Taking it to the head, it doesn't matter if anybody sees me.

"I'm gon' spank yo' butt lil' girl! Just cuz you just turned eighteen don't mean nothing." Squirrel creeps up behind me with his idle threat.

"Boy, I'm grown…You better not even try it, or I'm takin' this bottle to yo' big ol' head!"

With a chuckle, he takes the bottle and pours some in a red Solo cup. "Learn how to sneak man, damn." He gives me the cup and I buck the wine down in two sips. That's when I notice that creepy, old man is looking at me again.

"What's up with him?" Turning around, I refill my cup.

"I told you. Yo' mama work for him." Then he goes on to whisper in my ear that he owns a strip club.

My mouth falls open, but I'm not really surprised. The thing is, obviously she doesn't make much money, because she never has any. How can my father be okay with her doing that? The thought repulses me and that's why I know that I have to do whatever is necessary to get away from the horrible excuse I have for parents. If she is going to get money dancing naked for horny men, she should at least have something to show for it. Being a hoe isn't the worse thing a woman can do, but at least get your money stacked up.

The party is winding down. Most of my co-workers already left and now my family and friends are about to leave. The last two people to leave were Squirrel and my ex-boyfriend, Walter Green. After he realized that I was not giving him any play, he left.

* * *

It's now Monday and I'm back on that grind! Everybody is working really hard in the office and as usual, they start closing at 4:45 p.m. The intercom light flashes on my phone, so I pick it up. It is Dr. Lift.

"I need you to take dictation for a letter. Can you stick around for a few more minutes?"

"Sure, that's no problem Dr. Lift." Agreeing to stay, I say my goodbyes to the rest of the staff and lock the doors. A little voice in the back of my head tells me to set the alarm, so I do before going back to his office. He is sitting in his chair with his eyes cast down at something on his desk. This would be the perfect opportunity for me to do the doggone thing! Am I brave enough to be the one to make the first move? As I saunter around the desk, he greets me with a simple, "Thanks for staying back."

Turning his swivel chair around, I push his head back and plant a sultry kiss on his neck. Then I drop down to my knees. He doesn't protest as I unfasten his belt and slowly pull down his zipper. The entire time, I'm staring up at him seductively. Rocky is in for the ride of his life, because there is so much pent up aggression inside of me. Never did I know a man could scream so loud when he hit his climax.

"Ahh...Nae Nae...mmm...!" The pressure of his strong hand on the back of my head does not go unnoticed. He is so into it and as he moans, he grinds and thrusts.

"Arrgghh.... Yessss!" Dr. Lift bites down on his bottom lip and closes his eyes as he loses himself in the throes of pleasure. When I was finish making him my own personal snack, he pushes all his paperwork off his desk, bends me over and starts hitting it from the back.

All our clothes are piled on the floor; a hot mess. As I submit myself in the moment, I open up and take every inch of him. It is as if nothing else matters.

"Ohhh, Rocky..." My eyes roll back in my head as a powerful orgasm rocks my young body to the core. I'd never felt anything that incredible in my life.

"You feel so good...mmm..." His face is buried in my neck and when he releases his seeds on my back reality hits me. He did not use a condom, but thankfully I was on birth control just in case his pull-out method didn't work.

"Come on, let's go get cleaned up." We went to take a shower in the adjacent apartment and were at it again. *Nothing comes to sleep but a dream. Work hard for what you want,* and that's what I did. After we got dressed, his mood changed from passionate to demanding.

"You better keep your mouth shut little girl. I'm still married. No way will a few minutes of pleasure ruin my life. I've got a reputation to uphold."

Looking at him in disgust, I begin to defend my stance. "I'm no dummy, Dr. Lift!"

"Well, dummy or not, that is what I want from you." His otherwise calm, hazel eyes are wide.

"I might be an eighteen-year-old from the hood, but I *can* keep a dark secret." Faking a yawn, I tell him, "It's getting late and I don't want to get stuck in traffic."

"Nae-Nae, I still need you to take dictation for this letter."

"No! Have your head nurse do it in the morning!" He doesn't know how much power I have over him now! It's best he stays away from me! The sex was amazing, but the way he'd reacted right after just ruined the mood.

*   *   *

The next day, I go to work and just stay to myself. When I pass Dr. Lift in the hallway, he looks like he can crap his pants. With a smile, I keep on tending to my work. It is Friday night and everybody is on the way out of the office, leaving me alone with Dr. Lift again. I am clearing file folders off my desk, when I hear him call my name.

"Nae-Nae, in my office, *now!*"

What does he want with me?

"On my way, Dr. Lift. Let me lock up these folders."

Once I walk in his office, his smile gets broader and broader.

"You do know you're very sexy young lady? Eighteen and sexy!"

After clearing my throat, I speak up. "Well, they do call me *Pretty Chocolate*."

"I can see why. Bring your fine self over here!"

Rocky motions for me to come sit next to him. He pulls on my leg, indicating that he wants me to straddle him. Next thing I know, he is tugging and my shirt and pulling it over my head. By now, he's licking me all over my breasts and pulling down my pants. He is struggling with taking off his pants, so I just yank them down.

With my eyes on his, I say, "Rock my world…" He *owes* me that!

"You already know that's what I plan to do." With that said, he grabs each of my butt cheeks and squeezes before crushing my lips with his. When we are done, we take a nice, hot shower together. Rocky begins putting on his clothes. He is staring at the calendar on the wall with a big grin on his face.

"What's on your mind?" I ask as I put on my shirt? "It must be important. You're smiling, too!

"Have you forgotten, Nae-Nae? I'm taking you and my brother to dinner tomorrow."

"Oh snap! I totally forgot about that."

"I've got to go! I'll pick you up at 6 p.m."

The next day, Rocky is on time as promised. When I spot his brother, I can't help but think he is nice-looking too. Good genes run in their family. While we are sitting at dinner, Rocky's cell phone rings. A woman can be heard crying. After he ends the call, he explains.

"That was a patient. I'm so sorry." Then he asks his brother to drop me off at home.

His brother turns to look at me with a smile. "Nae-Nae, I brought you something," he brags. "My brother said you are going to school to be a plastic surgeon. It's a good field and it's not too shabby with the money. Before I drop you off, I'll just need to stop at my hotel room...to pick up your gift. Do you have a problem with that?" he questions. One thing I learned from mama was about body language. She said you could tell by body language if somebody's playing you. All I had to do was observe his behavior. Okay, check. What is he doing? He's tightly clutching his keys. That means he's nervous.

Rolling my eyes, I want to let him know I'm not some green, naïve little girl. How convenient. Why is my gift at the hotel? Couldn't he just drop it off at my house?"

After we get to his hotel room, I sit down in the chair closest to the door. If I need to make a break for it, I'm only a few feet from freedom. Rocky's brother is bald and clean-cut with a nice butt. Like his brother, he smells and looks great! He comes out with a purple box, with a silver bow. Attached is a note that reads: *If you are going to be a doctor, you must own a white lab coat.* After putting on the jacket and admiring myself in the mirror, I notice that my name is engraved on the upper left pocket. I reach out to give him a big hug. My hands end up traveling down to his butt! Then they move up and start rubbing on his shoulders. "You must exercise every day. Your muscles are so large and firm."

"How did you know? These muscles didn't come out of nowhere."

Maybe I should test the waters. His brother had pissed me off, so I grab him by the face and give him a deep kiss. His tongue spreads my lips and dances a sensual tango against mine. Then he takes his shirt and lifts it over his head. Planting soft, wet kisses on my neck, he reaches up my dress and gently pulls my panties down. And with that, he is on top of me, giving it to me raw! Both brothers know how to work a joystick!

"Ohhh…"

"Uhhh…"

"Mmm…"

"Ahhh…"

Our pleasure filled moans and the sound of skin against skin is all that can be heard up in that room. We have the windows fogging up in here, it is so steaming hot.

"Nae-Nae, care to join me in the shower?" He asks once we finally decide to come up for air. He has the sexiest, most irresistible smile!

"No, I plan on soaking in a hot bath at home. I need time to decide how I'm gonna deal with what just happened between us…" My voice is innocent as I look up at him.

"You do know that I'm married. With this type of scandal, I could lose my job and my wife."

I play stupid. Ladies, you can't let a man play you. It's a dog eat dog world, so eat, or be eaten.

"Really? Married, as in with a ring? I didn't see a ring on your finger."

"Can we keep this between us?" His eyes plead with me.

"Sure, we can." As I continue to play dumb, he breathes a sigh of relief. That's when I drop the bomb.

"Go grab your checkbook. My silence comes at the cost of ten grand."

"What? Are you freaking kidding me? Money like that don't come easy!" His eyes almost bug out of his head as his eyebrows furrow together in agony.

"Don't look so surprised…If you want to play the single game, you have to pay. Did you really think I was giving my kitty away for free? Breast implants cost a grip and it's not coming out of my pocket. You were the one who set yourself up. Talking about come to your hotel room to get a gift. I got my gift too. Joke's on you…sucka. Now, who got played?"

He picks his pants up off the floor and pulls out his checkbook and a ball point pen.

"Who should I make it out to?" He asks as his foot taps against the carpeted floor in frustration. I start to say *Pretty Chocolate*, but catch myself and give my real name. "It's Reginae Arnold!"

"Please don't tell my brother," he begs pitifully. He and his brother must both have a closet loaded with secrets. Sleeping with me is one of many, I was sure! If he only knew exactly how many skeletons would fall out of his brother's closet!

He dropped me off at the house around 10 p.m. Rocky called me around 10:15 to see if everything was cool. "I'm fine. Just want to go to sleep. It's getting late." Who knew…that for twenty minutes of loving, I'd be $10,000.00 richer. My graduation from high school is the following week. Without help from my mama or daddy, I manage to graduate with honors. The next day, I go to the bank with all the money from my mattress to open a checking and savings account. When I get back from the bank, I decide to tell mama and daddy that I am moving out, Apparently, that pisses them off. They are both standing near the front door, blocking my exit.

"What are you going do for money, baby?" My mama is crying." It's expensive to live in California. It's hard for me at my age…I shudder to think about an eighteen-year-old".

"For one, I won't be as trifling as you. How can you live on lousy tips from a strip club? At least own the club! Yes, I know what you do for a living! No need to hide it now!"

"Baby, that's all I could do for fast money. It's not like I have a formal education." She says that as if I should feel some type of pity for her.

Shaking my head, I say, "If nothing else, you taught me how to hustle."

Then, my daddy has the nerve to speak up.

"Now that you graduated from high school, will you still get that check once a month?" That poor excuse for a man can't even look me in the eye.

"Maybe, you should get a *real* job, daddy! Don't you think?" With my hand on my hip, I sass him with a menacing look in my eyes.

Back in my room, I start packing up my stuff. When I am finished, I call Portia to come get me. It takes her less than five minutes to get there.

"Girl, have you lost your mind?"

"No, I'm out of this dump… It's long overdue!"

"Girl, what side of town are you moving on?"

"Girl, you'll see. I'm tired and ready to go."

In no time, we are at my new apartment and I am so elated to have my own spot.

"I'll help you," Portia says.

"Okay, let's get these boxes."

Shaking her head, she tells me, "I can't believe it! Your mama and daddy were just sitting on the couch watching TV. Are they even affected by your leaving?"

"I couldn't care less, Portia. Can you grab my soda out the fridge?"

"Dang, girl! This is the most food I've ever seen in your fridge."

I will always have food! Never will I starve again.

The next day, I return to get the rest of my belongings and give my key back to my mama, before kissing her goodbye. After Portia drops me off at my new apartment, I treat myself to a relaxing bath in the garden tub. Relaxing on my bed, wet and naked, I can't help but think about how great life is. Finally, I have my own space. Then my phone starts to ring. When I answer, there's a woman screaming and cursing at the top of her lungs.

"If you go back to my husband's clinic, I will beat your lil' young tail like you mama should have!"

Then, I hear Rocky in the background. "Chill! It's not even what you think it is. It only happened once!"

"I don't give a damn!" His wife screamed before the call abruptly ended.

All I can do was sit there and think about what my actions could result in. It wasn't hard at all to admit, that it was all worth as I looked around at my spot. Forget that witch and her husband.

On Monday morning around eight, the sound of the phone ringing wakes me up from my peaceful slumber. Honestly, I'm not losing any sleep at all over Rocky and his jealous wife. It is Rocky calling. "Age Ain't Nothin' But a Number" is my special ringtone for him. The call drops when I answer, so he calls right back. This time, his voice is raspy yet firm.

"You might not want to come back to the office for real. I did not know my wife had hidden cameras installed. She got us on video. I know you're starting college in the Fall. I've already put in a good word for you with that professor I know at the University. Just don't come back to the clinic. Understand that it's all good."

Without saying anything further, I simply hang up. What he doesn't know is, I didn't plan to go back anyway.

A few weeks later, I receive a summons in the mail for me to go to court. By now, I'm in college. School is going very well and I have a part-time job as a barista at a coffee shop. I could be held in contempt of court if I didn't appear. The name on the summons is Rocky's wife, Mrs. Lift.

That puzzled me? Why did I have to go to divorce court? That is their marriage and I'd done what she asked by staying away. Upon my arrival, Rocky and his wife are standing across from me. The judge asks me to approach the witness stand.

"Is your name *Pretty Chocolate*?" The dark skinned, female judge with a short haircut looks at me like she wants to say, I know your real name! "Ms. Arnold, I need it for the record. Do you know why you're here?"

"Reginae Arnold. No, I have no idea your honor." By this time, I am rolling my eyes.

"You see that man standing over there?" She points with a non-nonsense look on her face.

"Yes, that's my former boss, Rocky Lift. What about him?"

This judge was not having it with my pettiness and nonchalant attitude. For a second, I thought she was about to step down from the bench!

"Look, little girl! According to the law you're an adult, but you better watch your tone in my courtroom. This is my house. You got it?"

"Yes, your honor." My eyes cast down in shame.

She goes on to explain that Rocky's wife had been going to a therapist three times a week and that it was because of our affair.

The bailiff walks over to the bench and she tells him something that we can't hear. He then walks over to a television screen and presses some buttons. The video of my romp with Dr. Lift was on full display. I almost laugh out loud, but I catch myself. I'd already tried it with the judge and didn't want to get locked up for contempt.

"Is that you in the video, Miss Arnold?" The judge stares down at me as she asks.

"That's me, your honor. A moment in time. It's old news now."

"Well, Mrs. Lift thinks otherwise. She feels that you should pay half of the bills for the therapy that was the result of your actions with her husband."

By now, I'm about to let everyone in this courtroom have it! Are you crazy? Pay what? Why didn't her husband pay it? It took two to tango and as I recalled, he was clearly there getting it in with me in that video.

"I'm going to order restitution. You must pay half of her medical bills along with you paying the other half Dr. Lift. It's the least you two can do. She's been seeing a therapist for three months. Your lesson for today Miss Arnold is, if you think a man can *rock* your world, make sure he's single."

Wow! What a stiff price to pay for my own pleasure and selfishness! All I wanted to do was get out of my parents' house and be engulfed in my own carnal pleasures at the same time. At first it seemed to be a win, win situation, but now that my hindsight was twenty, twenty, not so much. It was time to just put on my big girl panties and call it a day!

After I paid the restitution, I left both Rocky and his brother alone. Portia ended up moving in with me. I distanced myself further from my parents, since we didn't really talk much anyway. My cousin Squirrel was shot and killed doing his dirt in the streets, so my uncle moved away to Florida. Me, Reginae, aka, Nae-Nae, aka *Pretty Chocolate*, made it through four years of college. That recommendation from Rocky Lift came to me as promised. I went on to become one of the top plastic surgeons in Hollywood, California. I vowed that day in court to never let a man get the best of me. If anything, I was going to always come out on top.

VOWS DON'T MATTER

(For a Single Woman)

For better or worse; for richer or poorer; in sickness and health; till death do us part. Many of you have said these marriage vows...maybe once, or twice in your lifetime. Does anybody really know what it really means to *be* married?

Sleeping in, sex on-demand, his and hers sinks...you know... the usual that comes with the ball and chain! Growing up, I watched both of my parents work diligently to see that I never wanted for anything! Now, I, *the* fabulous Angel Hook, didn't grow up with my behind plastered to a 24-karat gold toilet seat. My father, Mr. Chase Hook worked as the head custodian at a posh hotel in downtown San Diego. He never went to college because he was dead-set on supporting *his* family. He was definitely a stand-up guy! Had he gone to college and graduated with his engineering degree, the struggle wouldn't have been so real. All he does now is fix air-conditioners and toilets! I know, what a life, right?

For the last two years, my dad has been sick and back and forth to the hospital. It's a challenge, so I wonder how I will make it through the next four years of college.

My mother, Mrs. April Hook, drives a school bus for a private Christian high school. After she finished high school, she did one year of college. All her dreams were canceled when I came in the picture, since she projected all that she loved upon me. My mother put me in cheerleading, modeling school, acting classes and had me prancing around in beauty pageants. Now, I did like that because it gave me an opportunity to meet lots and lots and lots of boys!

Let me get off memory lane and back into reality!

High school has been over for me! Can you believe I'm now in my senior year in college? Times are a little hard. My father and mother told me to find a part time job to help them with my tuition expenses. That kind of pisses me off being that I'm their one and *only* child… and I didn't ask to be spoiled. Don't they understand that I've only had one job in my life and that was at a swanky shop in downtown San Diego. The job satisfied my desire for expensive things.

One day, while relaxing in my dorm room, watching television, in walks my roommate Lucinda aka Luscious. She's a feisty, yet funny chick. Luscious is the one I owe for breaking me out of my shell. The girl once had her boyfriend Tony hide in my bed, take off his boxers and remain still until I got in. She knows that I sleep naked every night. As I slid underneath the covers, I felt a warm body. It did feel nice though.
Then, I was like, "Hey! What is this?"
You already know. Out pops Luscious from the closet laughing her head off.
"You need to experience a real man!" Her expression was priceless and I am sure mine was too.
I'll never forget that day!
She's always thinking about making those dollars and asked me if I wanted to make some *real* legit cash! The thought of money filling my pockets had me salivating.
Luscious brags, "Girl, now you can get that Brazilian hair you've been wanting."
"Yes, chick, let's get this money!" I'm all in.
"Here's the deal. What I'm about to tell you, you can't tell a soul. I'm only telling you because I can trust you and we have built a tight bond between us. Just think about making anywhere between five hundred to five thousand dollars a night just by going on dates with men. Let me be honest. You might have to do *more* than just go on a date!"

"Whaaat? What the hell you mean by a lil' more than a date? Like how much more? Please explain."

Luscious goes on to say, "Well, you might have to get on yo' knees and get a little grimy and don't wear no panties!

"Whaaat? Are you talking about being a prostitute?" My face seems to frown up on its own.

"No, girl I'm about that escort life! Fix yo' face! Don't judge me!"

"Whoa! I'm sorry. This is a lot to take in. I'm gonna have to think about it. I know I don't have much cash for school, but damn, I don't wanna sell my body for it either! This is way too much info to take in at one time! Gimme a few days and I'll get back with you. But, hypothetically speaking, if I do decide to do this…what's in it for you?"

"What do you mean what's in it for *me*? I'm tryin' to put cash in your pockets! Just sleep on it and get back with me in a couple of days. And, if you say yes, I'll give you page-by-page details."

Luscious doesn't know it, but I am already convinced and ready to work.

* * *

Luscious

It's Thursday and I still haven't heard anything from Angel about my proposition. Maybe she decided not to do it! I'm just trying to help her get this money like I got it! Or, maybe she's just scared. I hope she didn't tell on me though. I am going to give her one more day. If she doesn't bring it up, I will.

* * *

Angel

Why am I up at three in the morning thinking about money? Probably because I need some. Luscious didn't know the half of my worries and struggles. Even though we're roommates, I don't share a lot. Luscious looks so peaceful sleeping. Why does she have a Hello Kitty comforter like she's five, or something? Should I wake her up? I guess so.

"Wake up, Luscious! I got something to tell you!"

Rubbing the sleep from her eyes groggily, she asks, "Why you wake me? What's up? Is everything okay. Is something wrong?"

"No, girl! We good! I wanted to tell you I'm in. Let's get this paper!"

"Really, Angel? You ain't scared?" She has a skeptical look on her face.

"Nah, chick," I assure her.

"Meet me tomorrow morning at the Smoky Lounge at eight am on the dot. Don't be late. I'll give you all the details then. Dress real sexy and make sure you wear some stilettos! Sooo, you sure you ready? Cuz you gotta put yo' big girl drawers on for this. Are you 'bout that life?"

"Hell yeah," I say up for the challenge.

Unable to sleep, my nerves are wrecked wondering why I'm about to do this. Having a friend drop me off at the spot, I have second thoughts as we pull into the parking lot. Can I really do this? The butterflies that flutter in the pit of my stomach are a sign of how nervous I am. But then, I begin to think about those pesos that I am going to make, so I pull myself together, get out the car and thank my friend for the ride. Luscious is standing near the entrance with a smirk on her face.

"Dang, chick! That's a bad dress. That's gon' make them give you those dollars girl!" She shrieked, grabbing my hand to lead the way. "You definitely gon' have 'em droolin'!"

"You think so?"

"Heck yeah, chick! Let's walk!"

"Dang, I thought you said it was 'round here?" Staring to really get cold feet, part of me wants to turn around.

"Nah, it's 'round back! When we walk in, just be calm. I got you! Oh yeah, one more thing, Angel, never ever let the client kiss you in the mouth. When you get done with your date, you must check back in with Ms. C. The driver will drop you back off at the office, so you can get paid after you turn in all the money. Ms. C. will get 25% of your $1,000.00 for hooking us up with these millionaires. She always makes sure we are safe. That's why our limo driver named Johnny is always strapped. You never know what can pop off without a moment's notice."

Luscious and I haven't been in the place two minutes when a man that's about 6'3, chocolate, looking like Idris Elba, locks eyes with me and walks over to introduce himself.

"Wow! You must be new. I've never seen you before. You're breathtaking! One day, if you'll allow me, can I to take you to dinner?"

"Sure! Take my number."

Pulling his phone out, he punches the number in as I recite it.

"Hope to hear from you, sooner than later," I flirt.

"Oh, it will definitely be soon!"

The man walks away from me and begins to mingle with the other men.

Luscious walks over to me and I begin to tell her about the sexy chocolate man who spotted me from across the room.

"For real, Angel? Already? Dang! I'm jealous! Show me who he is!"

"It's him right there." As I point, I continue. "The one in the gray suit and red tie!"

"Him? For real? Oh my God! Do you know who that is? That is *the* husband of the HWIC, Ms. C Aka Control. His name is Marcus!" Luscious exclaimed.

"Whaaat?" This is surprising.

"That's who you are interviewing with."

"Whaaat? I got this...this is gonna be a breeze!"

My nerves are all jacked up as I'm walking towards the office. What does he expect from me? Knowing that he already likes what he sees doesn't seem to make it any easier for me. Before I can grab the doorknob, he stops me.

"I want you for myself. You gonna belong to me. No one else can have you. Do you think that's possible?"

"Me? Why me?"

"It's something about you that I like. You're young, but classy…and I can work with that. So how 'bout that dinner?" Those nice, bedroom eyes of his are capturing.

Taken aback, I ask, "When?"

"Tonight."

"Sounds like a date, but I don't even know your name? Who are you?" "I'm simply Marcus. My wife, Ms. C. runs the day operations, but I'm *the* man behind the woman. She's gonna send you on a date with my colleague first to let him *test* the waters and see if you're trustworthy."

"Well, Marcus I am a little nervous. I've never done this before." This is so weird.

"It's going to be like riding a bike, no need to be nervous. How about this. He is not a broke man. He owns an oil field. The driver will be here soon to take you to him."

Not able to hold in my laugh, I say, "It looks like I'm going to make some big money tonight."

Waiting on the driver has my feet hurting. Who wears six-inch high heeled stilettos? I do. And this damn dress is short as all get out. He better be pleased, or else! And where is this driver?! The life of the rich and famous…I digress! Who is that pulling up to the curb, driving that black Lincoln town car? It's nice. I wonder if it's my driver, Johnny. A short dark-skinned black man wearing a pale blue suit who reminds me of a young Kevin Hart steps out of the limo and approaches me.

"You must be Ms. Angel Hook! Ms. C told me a little about you. Let's go. We can't keep the client waiting!"

"Yes, I'm Angel and you're Johnny, right? Ms. C. don't play when it comes to being prompt I see."

"Nope! She's one tough woman to work for. Tough but fair."

As Johnny pulls up to the art museum, he points at the crowd. "Look at all those important people and you are one of them. Are you ready for this, Ms. Angel?"

"I'll try my best," I mumble.

Johnny gets out of the limo and goes around to open my door like a gentleman. He gives me a picture of the client that is meeting me at the exhibit and tells me that the client has *all* details on me including my age, height, weight and boob size.

Wow! This man knows all about me! It's kind of creepy.

"When you see him approach him. His name is Stefan Hardwick."

"He's 6'3 and weighs about one ninety. His favorite color is baby blue." Johnny even ran down what kind of car he drives and his favorite two colognes. It was like he was giving me his personal resume. I already know that he owns his own oil field, so that is a plus.

"Work your smile! Show off those seductive legs! We call him Stefan H. Aka *Always Has a Hard On*. Show him what your mama gave you."

"Ms. C. told me you had big boobs." Johnny chuckles. "Stefan loves ladies with big boobs." Johnny drops me off at the front door before handing me a business card with his cell number on it. He reassures me that he isn't going anywhere.

"My job is to wait on you and watch out for your safety." He also reminds me that he has a license to carry and stays strapped. "I'm trained with this 9 mm and will not hesitate to use it to keep you safe."

As I walk up to the door of the art museum, I'm mesmerized. Going inside, I take in the beautiful art that adorns the walls. I am standing in front of a portrait, studying its abstract beauty, when I notice a good-looking man standing next to it. We make brief eye contact. Could this be the client? It is *the* Stefan Hardwick. We can't keep our eyes off each other. We just keep staring and staring into each other's eyes. He is very well-dressed, wearing an expensive Italian suit. Clearly, he's a man of impeccable taste. Then, I have a flashback of my childhood years. My parents could never afford those clothes, or sunglasses. Oh, my! Rare Vintage! They cost about $5,000! Back in my high school days, that price stuck in my memory while working at an upscale sunglass boutique. Now I'm glad those days are behind me.

Looking at Stefan from head to toe, I mutter to myself, 'I want me some him!' He has on alligator skin shoes and his initials are inscribed in his cufflinks "S & H." At that point, I declare, 'This man is going to be my husband.' But there is one catch. He has a wedding ring on his left finger. *Vows don't matter*…I want this man. And from that day forward, I will make it my mission to get him. We both are standing and admiring a painting by the great Leonardo da Vinci.

Stefan reaches out, grabs my hand and kisses it. "You must be Ms. Angel…I recognize the picture that Ms. C. sent over to me. What a beautiful lady." He immediately starts complimenting my dress with his eyes glued to my big boobs. I am working that mini dress!

Stefan snickers, "Ms. C. really knows my tastes." We both casually start walking to the next exhibit.

"What do you mean about that?"

Licking his lips, he says in a low, enticing voice, "You're just my type; sexy, smell heavenly and that dress fits you like a glove!" Then, Stefan starts mumbling something in French. I don't understand him, but simply say thank you in English. We walk around the art museum for another forty minutes and look at the exhibits.

"Will you like to have dinner? I made reservations for us at a restaurant that is right next door. I'd never take you to a restaurant that is not five stars. Breathing a sigh of relief, I say, "Thank you!" Unable to control the grin on my face, I'm in pure bliss! I need to gather myself and hip Johnny to what is going on.

"I have to go step outside for a second." Calling Johnny, I tell him that we are about to have dinner next door. He assures me that he'll be waiting on me.

"Now get back to your client."

"Hey, you," Stefan whispers in my ear when I walk back inside causing chills to travel down my spine." You like Greek food?"

"Yes, I love it."

"What is it that you like, Angel? Me, I'm all for the belly dancers." Stefan chuckled.

"Give me *all* the desserts, especially the baklava," I quip.

"Well, Angel feed me *all* the desserts, all of them!" As he winks, I lick my lips just to toy with him.

"It would be my pleasure," I promise.

As Stefan grabs my right arm and wraps it around his left arm, he insists that a beautiful woman like me needs a bodyguard. "I'm *it* for the night. I will protect that beautiful body!"

I am not opposed. If he gets any closer to me, I will be *on* fire!!!

The citrus and wooden smell of his Issey Miyake cologne is making me so wet my panties are sticking to me. Feeling myself melt into his arms, I don't want the night to ever end. Stefan has a great personality and great conversation. It's like we've been friends for years. We just click.

The walk to the restaurant is only three blocks down the street, so it is nice and short. We both are getting to know each other by asking general questions. He tells me about his family and I tell him about my parents. Neither of us bring up the subject of him being obviously married. When we arrive, I realize the restaurant is empty, except for the staff. We are the only customers in the restaurant.

"Where is everybody?" Stefan states that he does not want to be disturbed, so he paid for the restaurant for the night. He did it just for me.

"I can afford the finer things."

I'm in utter and total disbelief.

Reassuring me that he has everything under control, he says, "This night is going to be perfect."

The hostess leads us to our table and we both sit down. I'm admiring the table and the candlelight. As Greek music plays, seven beautiful women come out dressed in pink and green belly-dancing garb. Stefan seems to be in a trance, watching these women move their hips rapidly. As their boobs jiggle, I notice drool coming from the side of his mouth. This guy is really into boobs! He reaches out and smacks one of the girls on the butt as she passes by him. The belly dancer gives him an, "if you do that again, I'll slap you" stare. Wanting to laugh, I maintain my composure. Receiving a text from Ms. C, I see that she wants to know how the date is going? Responding back, I quickly send her a happy face and dancing emoji.

Stefan puts his hand on the small of my back and says, "I'm itching to have you see this gorgeous painting that I have, since you are into art."

He's going on and on about it, so I agree to go see the painting, but we have to go back to his hotel. He insists on *his* driver taking us there.

"I need to excuse myself to the ladies' room."

That time I call Johnny to let him know that the plans are changed.

"I'm headed to Stefan's hotel and I will call you when I'm ready to go home."

Stefan thanks the staff and leaves a handsome tip for each server. On the way to the hotel, Stefan can't keep his hands off me. It is like his hands are glued to my anatomy. It really doesn't matter. He is very well-educated, handsome and sexy, so I don't mind.

After taking the elevator to the 20th floor, he walks with me hand in hand to his penthouse. Walking inside of the luxuriously elegant space, I notice how lovely it is decorated. Stefan pats the seat next to him.

"Come!"

Walking over to a table, he grabs something and turns around. He has some pink roses and a box of chocolates in his hands.

"This is for you pretty lady! You deserve this and more!" He walks over to a safe and pulls out a long, black leather case.

Removing the painting from the case, he explains, "I got it from an auction today. It's a one-of-a-kind, original black and white sketch portrait by Renoir." The illustration is of a woman bathing in a tub. And you guessed it! She has big boobs. He offers me a glass of wine, claiming that he *knows* everything about me. Whatever! I'll let him *think* that!

We exchange some small talk about him relocating from Los Angeles to San Diego. On top of being an oil man, he's also a corporate lawyer. "Business is expanding. I'm about to close on a mansion that has ten bedrooms."

Whoa! What does one person need with that many rooms? That's none of my business though.

He makes it very clear that he wants to see me again. "I'm looking forward to that call from Ms. C."

I'm starting to fall for this guy! Who wouldn't? He's good-looking, smells mmm mmm mmm good and he's a millionaire! I could have the perfect life if this man could be my husband! I could be Mrs. Stefan Hardwick! Now those relationship goals are on fleek!

How can I get his wife out the picture? Send her fake ultrasounds?

No. Oh, Ok! I got it! The first time we sleep together, I'll wait about a month and then give him news that I'm pregnant. That should get him. This is only a *one-time* thing because Luscious had coaxed me into it. Why am I entertaining the thought of another date?

Stefan casually placed ten crisp hundreds in my palm. Yes! Not wanting to show my excitement, I held it in. He walks me to the door, gives me the biggest hug, and then tries to kiss me on my lips. Recalling what Luscious told me, I quickly turn away so he'd miss my lips. His lips land on my nose. We hug and say our goodbyes.

Johnny is waiting for me at the door as I walk towards the curb. He opens the car door, helps me inside and then closes the door.

"How was the date?" Johnny questions.

"I really enjoyed it and he asked to see me again. A girl could get used to the royal treatment. Stefan really knows how to treat a woman."

"So, how much did he give you?" His eyes meet mine in the rearview curiously.

"Sorry sir, but I cannot disclose."

Johnny chuckles. There is a little note attached to the money. When we get to the office, I am given the chance to meet Ms. C Aka Control. She is an average woman. Nothing really to talk about. She seems very nice and friendly.

"I just got a call from Stefan. He really enjoyed you. He told me that he wants to see you next Thursday."

"Okay, well, I'll get back to you."

The next three weeks I am taking finals. I can't mess up now. I'm graduating in about four weeks. My parents will kill me if I flunk out now. After passing Ms. C. the envelope that Stefan gave me, she quickly takes out her twenty five percent and gives me the rest. It's mine, all mine. I cannot believe it! That was the best date ever!

"Angel, before you leave, let me talk to you." Her voice is stern, and direct. She seems to be slightly upset.

"Yes, Ms. C. Is everything alright?"

"You seemed to have made quite an impression on my husband, Marcus. He was going on and on about you. You know if you give him some, he'll just come back home to me! Daddy *always* comes home! Do we understand each other, Angel? Stay away!"

"Yes! Yes, Ms. C. I'll stay far away," I stammer.

Whew, boy am I glad to be out of that boiler room with Ms. C. I don't want her darn man, Marcus anyway! Stefan, now he's a true contender. Well, honestly he's the *only* contender, for my heart!" Johnny asks me if I am ready to go and I nod yes. He drops me off at my dorm's entrance.

Walking into the room, I notice that Luscious is still up.

"Angel, I have been waiting up for you. I wanted to see how your date went," she pries with a sly smile. "If you go on one date at least twice a week… you'll make bank really quick!"

"I was asked to go on date number two next Thursday!"

Luscious and I squeal in excitement.

"You're in the money now girl!"

The next day, we both wake up late. We rush to get to our classes, because it is time for final exams. I must admit, I can't get Stefan out of my mind. Thinking of him is making it really hard to concentrate. Class needs to be over now! As soon as I say that, the professor dismisses us because her little boy is sick. I'm working towards a BS in psychology. I've always wanted to get in people's heads to see what makes them tick. Gee! There are about fourteen missed calls from my mom! She is blowing my phone up! What's the deal? As soon as mom gets me on the phone, she holds me hostage.

"Angel, now I've called you several times! What's going on?" She groans. "Me and your father invested a lot of time and money into your future. I'm still working on getting that six thousand dollars before you graduate."

Wanting to tell my mom all about my new job, I lie and say that I am babysitting children of high profile millionaires near the school.

"How'd you luck up on that," she wonders.

I tell her, "A client's father was impressed with me when I helped his daughter calm down after McDonald's ran out of French fries. He said that I was a *child-whisperer* of sorts."

She is wholly impressed. "Well, you be safe. Even people with money can be crazy."

With a laugh I say, "I will. Love you too mama!"

* * *

Nobody in life is going to give you anything. You must take what you want! Look at that simple chick, Ms. C! Who is she? If she can get all these millionaires as clients, I can do the same. I decide that I will become a full-fledged madam and cut her out. You've heard the old saying, cut out the middleman. That's why I am going to start my own business. All my college friends are broke, so I'm sure they would love to work for me! Especially when they hear how much money they can make in one night.

Most of them would earn enough to pay off their tuition. I hope Luscious, will work for me. If she takes the part time job, I'll make her the head person in charge of the girls. Deciding to call Luscious and offer her the job, I ask her to pick me up so we can have a latte at our favorite coffee shop. Running down the stairs, I rush to Luscious' car and we greet each other.

"I'll pay for the food and drinks today."

Luscious looks at me cheesing "Wow! You must've had a good night! You're rolling in serious dough, honey!" We slap each other five.

"True that!" We pull up to a coffee shop called *Butterscotch* and sit down to order. Luscious orders herself a latte and I start laying out my business plan.

"We are both graduating in a couple weeks. Ms. C. makes a lot of money off us, so I am going to start my own business, like Ms. C. I want you to be in charge of the girls. I'll start you off with fifty dollars per hour for your time and when we start making money, I'll give you more."

"Are you serious, Angel! That old biddy would kill you!" She warns.

"Hell, yeah! When I'm done with school, this plan is going into *full* motion!"

"Who's your first client? It's not like you know any rich men?"

Our drinks are delivered and we both take much needed sips.

"Stefan! And, yes! He *always has a hard-on*...I felt it!"

"You got jokes, huh! That's Ms. C's number one client. Honey, you really got balls!"

"Are you in or not? Luscious, I need you! You'll make sure their makeup is on fleek, they have regular STD testing and ensure their safety! And, Johnny is coming with me too!"

"You are starting a war! Ms. C. is going to be so pissed off at you. You're going to need a bodyguard! If you're not careful, you'll be dead as soon as she finds out."

"I'm not worried about that old lady! She doesn't have a clue who I am!"

"You better go out and get a gun. You're going to need it."

"I don't think so! Let that old lady try to come after me. She gon' be checking into a nursing home really quick."

"Alright, Ms. Thang! Or should I call you, boss lady Angel!"

"That's fine, but just don't call me out of my name and I won't have to fire your behind!" We both start laughing in unison.

"I'm not going to bite the hand that feeds me," Luscious promises.

"This is my action plan. I need you to go around to all the girls' dorms. You must be very discreet and see how many girls want to make some fast cash working part-time for me. We gotta keep this hush-hush. That way, the Dean won't catch on before all of us graduate, or we'll get expelled from school."

Four years of college really made me feel like I don't want to work for anybody. Being my own boss seems more appealing. Luscious and I are going to put our plan in action tomorrow. Once we write everything down, I'll show Luscious how to quiz the girls. The first rule is to make sure they keep their mouths shut, the second rule is they must make a minimum three-day commitment, number three is they have to get regular STD testing, number four is they have to submit a five by seven headshot. We also need to have all the final details on all the girls. That way, we'll be able to match up our clients with the right kind of girls. The client can pick girls from our website.

"Angel Hook, you are brilliant! How did you become so smart?" Luscious is beaming at me all proud.

"I'm a psychology major, so shrink is in my blood! It's a rush to get into someone's head to try to figure them out."

"Girl, you are really good at this!"

"Remember, I'm done with school. I've got a whole new lease on life now."

"Damn, you should've been a business major boo!"

We finally leave the coffee shop and go back to the dorm to prepare for our finals. Not able to go to sleep, my mind is hard on Stefan. Oh, how I would love to take over his body. Deciding to text Stefan to tell him good night, I let him know I am looking forward to seeing him next Thursday. He texts me back a wine glass and a couple kissing emoji.

My heart starts to flutter. Stefan has indeed stolen my heart!

The very next day, Ms. C. calls to confirm my date with Stefan for next Thursday.

"Johnny will pick you up by five and your dinner date will start promptly at six."

Immediately ending the call, I say out loud to myself, "I hate when people try to control my life. Taking this old lady's business will be like pulling off a cheap wig; quick and painless." I laugh wickedly.

The week goes by very fast as me and Luscious get through our finals. Just one more week to go and then we will be graduating. We cannot contain our excitement! Luscious comes in from the library one night, "turnt" all the way up! She starts doing the Nae Nae dance and everything!

"Luscious, who poured a kilo of sugar in your tea? You lit girl!"

"Angel boo, I got the numbers of twenty girls. They all agreed to work for you part time. The headshots and resumes are on the way to your e-mail!"

"Fantastic! Everything is working in our favor!" A satisfied smile decorates my face.

"Don't you have a date with Stefan tonight?"

"Yes, he's taking me to his new house that he wants me to see."

With a frown Luscious asks, "Ain't he married? You wanna be wifey now?" Forming her hands into a megaphone, she shouts, "Men, watch out, she'll take your world!"

"Mama needs a new pair of shoes! Ha!"

All of a sudden, my instant messenger alarm starts sounding off. It states that there are twenty pictures in all.

"We'll be open for business as soon as we graduate!" Luscious gleams excitedly.

"I need to come up with six stacks in about a week. Stefan is good for the money. He owns a doggone oil field!"

"Do you really think he's going to give it to you?" Her face is filled with doubt.

"Honey, when I get through working that fine man's body, he will be begging me to take it! I'm gonna put it on him like no other! My body all over *his* body. His body all over *my* body!"

Frowning her face up, Luscious shrieks, "Huh? Isn't that a song by LSG? Stop! Stop! I don't want to hear all that!"

To make it easier for me, Luscious prints out all the pictures and lays them out side-by-side on the floor, so I can view them closely. She suggests that we go over all of them later that night when I got home.

"I'm sure I'll be too tired. We'll do it in the morning."

Johnny is on time as usual on Thursday. As I am about to get in the limo, another limo pulls up behind Johnny's. The other limo driver gets out of the car, walks around and opens the door. That's when I hear the familiar voice say, "Good evening, beautiful!" Instantly, I can feel myself getting hot, knowing that it is Stefan!

"Are you surprised? I wanted to pick you up so we can look at the house together!" There's a huge grin on his face that matches mine.

My heart is fluttering. "Stefan! This is a wonderful surprise! Johnny please let Ms. C. know what I'm doing and that I will get back with her tomorrow."

"Now, remember, you have to turn that money in to Ms. C's office *every* night," Johnny reminds me.

"Johnny, Ms. C. is no longer in control...I am!" The serious look on my face lets him know that I'm not playing.

So off Stefan and I go! Stefan slowly slides closer to me. This time, he reaches over to give me a kiss instead of a hug. Remembering Luscious' warning, I wiggle out of Stefan's embrace.

"What's wrong? Why won't you let me kiss you?" Stefan asks in disappointment.

"We'll have plenty of time for that! And, when I kiss you, you'll crave only my kisses!"

"Oh! you just trying to play hard to get, but I love the challenge!" Stefan grins slyly.

We pull up to the house and it reminds me of something I would only see in a magazine! Being with Stefan makes it picture perfect! Stefan begins giving me a tour. Marveling about the grand chandelier in the foyer and in the indoor swimming pool, I can picture myself living there. Pretending to listen, I insert *yeah* and *uh huh* in all the right places. This is the perfect time for my six-thousand-dollar pitch.

So, I start talking about my dad and his ever-increasing medical bills. The Academy should give me an Oscar for best lead actress in a major motion film.

Pulling my bottom lip over the top one, all my sad faces work. Stefan turns around, looks at me and pulls me close. "Sweetheart, I'm sorry to hear about that. What can I do to help?"

"To graduate, I need six thousand dollars to pay off my tuition."

"No problem! I'll take care of that! I'll do anything for you. That's my word."

"Anything?" I have to confirm.

"Yes, anything!"

At that moment, I want to see if he is serious. "Leave your wife! This should be my house!"

"Angel, do you believe in love at first sight? I'm in love with you!"

"You've captured my heart, Stefan…I love you, too!" My heart almost explodes with happiness.

"I want you now, Angel! Let's go back to the hotel. I want to make passionate love to you!"

Stefan grabs my hand. We walk outside and the driver drops us off at the hotel. Barely able to get in the room without ripping off each other's clothes, he passionately throws me on the bed. Then he climbs on top of on me and slowly starts kissing my body. He goes straight to my nipples before his tongue cascades down my inner thigh.

"Ohhh… that feels sooo good!" Not able to contain myself, I pull him up.

Our lips meet again. Both his lips and tongue satisfy my desire for his taste. Luscious told me never to kiss the client, but I could not help myself. This man is so sexy and he confessed that he loves me.

"I knew you'd feel this good. Mmm… I knew it when I first saw you." Stefan doesn't waste anytime savoring the taste of my tongue again.

"Mmm… baby… ohhh… Stefan… I love you…"

Stefan turns me around and enters me roughly from behind.

Screaming out in ecstasy, I look back at him seductively, watching as he long stroked me deeply.

"Mmm…. Ahhh…. Yessss…. Stefan… that's the spot!" My eyes roll back in my head as I throw it back at him like a real freak.

He's loving it and I can tell from the way he's grinding and moaning his pleasure.

"Arrrrgggghhhhh! You are so wet… Oh my god!" He groans in my ear and then sucks softly on my earlobe.

Flipping me on my back, he says, "I wanna look at you…" Entering me again, he's gentler this time. Feeling myself losing it, the shake in my leg is the first sign of my impending orgasm.

His strong hands were squeezing my butt cheeks and then he slapped each of them.

"I'm 'bout to…"

"Me too…" he says breathlessly.

We release all our pleasure at the same time and as we do our lips meet again. As he holds me in his arms, he promises he will never let me go. I wish this moment could be frozen in time.

"I plan to start my own business after graduation." Turning on my side, I look at him.

Looking back at me intently, he asks, "What type of business?"

My eyes widen as I speak confidently, "Just know, that Ms. C. will soon be replaced."

"Do you have a business plan? If you're serious, I'll sign on as your attorney."

"No, Stefan! A business plan for working as a madam? Yeah, right!" I laugh.

"Would you mind helping me start my private practice? I'm going to divorce my wife and make you mine. I'll have the movers gather your things from your dorm and my things from my home. They'll put everything in the new house for us."

"Oh, Stefan! I don't know what to say!" My giddiness couldn't be contained as I jump into his arms.

"Say yes, Angel! Please say yes! Your mom and dad can move in too."

"My father can help you around the house. He's a great fixer-upper."

"That's not necessary. I will hire a maid and a groundskeeper."

"Stefan, do you really love me?" My doubts have surfaced.

"Yes, Angel, I do!"

In his arms, I fell into a sound sleep. Visualizing our future and the life we would build together, it was the most peace I'd had in a while. And now, I'll be in his arms every night, forever and always!

The next morning his driver calls about eight in the morning to tell us he will be at the hotel in an hour. We both get up, take a nice hot shower and try to restart where we finished. Then we realize we have no time. While we are in the shower, he says to me, "Put everything in motion with your business. When I come back in town next week, we will start our new life together."

Stefan writes me out a check for twenty thousand dollars and tells me to use six thousand for my tuition.

"Give Ms. C. a thousand and keep the rest for your business."

"At this point I already have twenty girls lined up for my business."

"Wow, I'll email you a list of men who will be happy to use your services." Stefan advises me to handle his millionaire clients with care.

Stefan's driver takes me back to the dorm as I dream about all the money I will be making. When I get back to the dorm Luscious is in a panic. The minute I walk in the door, she warns me. "Girl, Ms. C. has been calling me looking for you!"

"Hmph! Why? Stefan had me all night!"

"Did you enjoy yourself? She's looking for her money. Johnny will be here in twenty minutes to get her cut. She demands that you call her immediately!"

After I dial her number, the phone rings about eight times before she picks up.

"Hello, this is Angel."

"How was your date? Stefan is very fond of you." Her voice is full of malice.

"It was great, Ms.C, as always!"

"Johnny's on his way for my cut. You know that's twenty five percent, as always! In a hurry, I run down to the ATM machine and take out two withdrawals of two fifty hundred. Johnny pulls up right after that. Now, it is my opportunity to offer him a job, so he can stop working for Ms. C.

"If you work for me, I'll double Ms. C's pay." He shakes my hand in agreement with not much coaxing than that.

By the time I get back to the dorm room, I sit down with Luscious. We start going over the pictures and narrow it down to fifteen girls. Luscious is to contact all of them and present them a schedule. It is getting late, so we go to bed.

My mom calls me early that morning. "Baby, I have to let you know that we aren't able to come up with the rest of your tuition."

Happily, I fill her in with part of the truth, "I received a scholarship to cover it. It was granted to me due to dad's illness."

$$* \quad * \quad *$$

On graduation day that following Monday, Luscious and I take pictures with our fifteen newfound employees. We are all excited about making money! This is the stuff only dreams are made of!

On Wednesday, I let the movers in to arrange the furniture in the new house I share with Stefan. He is due to arrive back in town on Saturday. Stefan is truly a man of his word. He did leave his wife for me and we started our businesses together. He is a private practice attorney and I am a madam. Stefan and I have become successful and we make a lot of money. Ms. C. aka Control went out of business and I took all her clients. Johnny is our limo driver and business is so good, I had to hire an additional five drivers.

My mom and dad met Stefan and decided to move in with us. My father quit his job and stays home due to his health, while my mother works part-time and takes care of him during the day. Luscious got her degree in education and three months later, she and Tony got married. She still works part-time for me. The lesson here is, if you marry, you better do everything possible to keep your man, otherwise a single woman will take your world.

SHE'S A REAL COUGAR

You never know who you'll meet at the airport! From that fine actor John Stamos to a host of R&B's artists, I've seen them *all*. Allow me to introduce myself. My name is Ms. Janelle Love. I'm a flight attendant based out of MIA and I work for one of the largest airlines in the world. MIA is airport code for Miami, FL. Pay attention, because I'll be using those frequently As hair-raising as turbulence is in the air, so are snippets of my life, so let me share! I had a very bad breakup after my husband passed away. I'm alone by choice. Yes, forty-one years old, insatiable and three years without a man! Right now, you can just say... I'm celibate

Curtis had a stroke while we were making love. Imagine the horror on my face, not to mention the Cheshire cat grin on his. Guess you can say I have a *lot* of energy. My husband was a great provider and a hardworking man. I wanted for nothing! He slaved fifteen years for a railroad company, only to miss retirement because of his untimely death.

We both decided at a young age that we did not want *any* children, so we never had any. So, now I'm in this house with no kids, no dog, no cat, no plants, and last, but not least, no husband, *or* boo. Pretty sad, huh? Can I at least have a parrot, or something? Well, that's what my sister Lisa would suggest. Family is something I *do* have.

Born and raised in Miami, Florida, I was destined to be the go-to counselor for *everyone*, since I'm the eldest of my four siblings. My father was a pilot and my mother was a flight attendant. That's how they'd met. Not long after that, they had me. They both are retired now. You could say that it's in my blood to be in the air. I have two sisters and one brother. Lisa is the one after me and worked as an OB/GYN, LaToya, the baby girl is an attorney with her own private practice and my only brother, Teddy, is a professional basketball player who plays overseas. He is sponsored by Game Time Academy. Me and my siblings are very successful in our respective careers. It's great to be on my way from MIA to HOU. Yes, I'm using airport code again. I'm sure you figured out that HOU is Houston, Texas. As I check my schedule for the next few days, I see that I only have a two-day trip! It's Friday and I'm leaving MIA to do an overnight in HOU, and then going to ATL on Saturday morning. Then, I'll be doing a turn around and going right back to MIA the same day.

I pray that when I get to ATL there is not any IROP. Sorry! That means irregular operations due to rain, or mechanical problems. If it rains, I will be spending the night in an ATL hotel and not in *my* bed! Boo hoo! Starting to put on my flight attendant uniform, I stop midstream. I'm vain, so I didn't want to mess up my hair and makeup.

Ladies, you can relate if you're forty-one and over. It's no joke! I have my own private little summers, sweating so profusely you'd think I'm in a sauna. I refuse to take the pills! Can you say the diva's all decked out for work? My hair is looking nice and my makeup is *flawless*. Wow, I'm slaying for real! Let me get going! Grabbing my cell phone, I call my sister LaToya. She does not pick up. After leaving her a voice message, I decide to text her. She still does not call me back, but is considerate enough to text me.

Latoya: Girl, can't drop you off at the airport today. I'm meeting with a new client in my office … right at this moment. Sis, you should meet my client. ☺This *young* man is good looking and got his own swag... smells good, too. Mmm...a young *tenderloin*. LOL.

Me: I don't want no broke man! He gon have to be Captain or First Officer because that's where the money is at.

My sister texted me back.

Latoya: Sis you betta stop texting me and get yo butt to the airport, girl! You don't want to miss your flight!

After getting dressed real fast, I run out the door and jump in my car. I'm rushing out of my driveway when I see my neighbor outside gardening. Her name is Ms. Lucy. She's always reminding me that I am ALWAYS late for work. Don't I know it! Ms. Lucy needs a life and to mind her own business! With a smirk on my face, I still tell her good morning.

My new car is a gray, fully loaded Porsche that pulls out of my driveway in 2.5 seconds! I love my car! It is no joke. This bad boy gets up! Driving toward the park and ride, I see the shuttle in front of me. Putting the pedal to the metal, I pass the shuttle. So happy I made it to the park and ride before the shuttle pulled up. I can't help but think it is going to be a good day. That was a close call! I will not be doing that again. Can you say time management? Yes, I need to do better. Can't see myself getting fired now, especially after investing fifteen years of my life into that company. They don't care how long you've been with them, they will fire your behind with the quickness. My girl, Tiffany, saved me a seat as I settle down to the addictive sound of "Earned It" by The Weeknd coming from my headset. Listening to him always has me fantasizing about this pilot, Captain Cecil S. Mmm… the things I could do to him behind closed doors! He ain't ready!

We pull up to the airport on time. Then we all get off the shuttle and start walking inside. All four of the flight attendants go to the gate at the same time and are informed by the gate agents that we must wait for the captain and first officer. The first person that shows up is the first officer, Sean M. He starts working on the passenger list, because it is not ready. Oh my gosh! All that rushing I did to get to the airport and the gate is not ready? Now, the two gate agents have pissed me off and I'm not very happy! This day is making me feel a little discombobulated. Turns out I was wrong, because my day has already taken a turn for the worse.

The female gate agent said to the first officer, "Go ahead and do your plane inspection. I know you have to walk around the plane thoroughly and inspect it before you get on board. The paperwork will be sent to you when it's ready."

First officer Sean M. left the gate, went on the plane to complete his inspection.

Next thing I know, the female gate agent says, "Flight attendants, you can board the plane now. It's ready."

One of the gate agents starts to walk towards the door with the passenger list. Noticing that the strap on my shoe is loose as I'm walking towards the gate door, I bend down to tighten it before I get on the plane. As I get up, out of the corner of my left eye, I catch a glimpse of a man walking toward me. Slightly turning to my left, I wonder what is that smell? Yesss! That's Jimmy Choo Man. Honeydew melon and pink pepper. The nose never lies. How do I know? Because, I used to buy that for my husband from Macy's'. Oh, my goodness! It's him! The Captain Cecil S. II had a caramel complexion, 6'2 with dimples. Damn, baby's fine! It is a delight to see to him at my home base, the MIA, FL airport.

Captain Cecil S. II walks past me and looks me straight in the eye, while getting on the plane. He parts those sexy lips to say, "Good morning!"

My eyes are deadlocked on those lips. Can I get a kiss? Those lips are too damn juicy! Every single solitary time I see him, he makes my body talk. Thinking of him gets me *super wet*. If these Victoria's Secret panties could talk, what would they say? "Go wipe that kitty dry."

Chuckling, I know I need to take a moment to handle that. After asking Fernando, one of the flight attendants to cover me, I scurry off to use the restroom. Soon as I get in there, I hurry to take off my blouse and grab some paper towels to wipe down my body and face. Then I use more paper towels to wipe down and cool my overheated kitty cat.

That man has me so hot and turned on. But I must snap back into reality, put my blouse back on and get back to work.

Once I put my blouse on and leave the bathroom, guess who it is I see? Rhonda aka Rude! She's sooo obnoxious! We exchange a few pleasantries. You know, the usual, "How're you doing today" type of stuff. It's hard to concentrate on working with this sexy good-looking man distracting me. A woman couldn't help but have full-fledged X-rated movies roaming through her mind about him!

Well, all four flight attendants are on the flight. Rhonda aka Rude is the lead flight attendant and that makes me *very* happy! That smart mouth wench is always getting on my last nerve! I know one thing, if she says anything out of line to me, my facial expression should jolt her mouth shut! She *will* know that I'm pissed off!

Today we are on a 757 flight, which accommodates a lot of passengers. I'm so happy we are not on a M90 today. After all that rushing and trying to get to work, I'm a little worn out. Positioned at the front door, my assignment is to work the first-class passengers. I love it! Starting things off on the right foot, I greet all the passengers with a hearty good morning as they are walking on to the plane. Flashing my pretty, big smile, they smile and nod in return. Everyone is almost onboard as we start to do our announcements. One of the gate agents walks on the plane and asks me to watch over a ten-year-old boy who is unaccompanied. Unaccompanied means that an adult is not traveling with an underage child between the ages of five years to fourteen years old.

They must be enrolled in this program called Unaccompanied Minor. It's the parents' choice after the child turns fifteen years of age if they want them to continue in the Unaccompanied Minor program. Once they reach the age of fifteen they can freely fly by themselves without an adult, domestically or internationally, without the program instated.

"The airlines will not be at fault," we say in unison.

"This service is not free, or cheap. They have to pay each way if they're traveling on a round trip ticket," I point out. "We have to do excellent work and not lose these little kids, although some are brats." We start laughing at the same time.

"Will you take over this paperwork and sign off on the unaccompanied, Ms. Janelle?" The agent begged. "I want this plane to takeoff on time."

Then I ask the other flight attendant, Fernando D. Aka Dog, if he will finish greeting the rest of the first-class passengers, because I have to walk the unaccompanied minor to the back of the plane. He gives me a thumb's up!

The accompanied minor is a ten-year- old a little boy named Isaiah who has black, curly hair. He is so adorable! Starting to make small talk with him, I ask, "Who are you going to see in Houston?"

"I'm visiting my dad and grandma who are flying in from Atlanta. My auntie also lives in Houston." This kid is so excited to see his family. His dad promised him a new bike and his auntie is taking him on a shoe shopping spree. I wish I was this kid!

When I reach the back of the plane, I hand Isaiah off to Rhonda R. She and Rachel F. Aka Forgetful, are working the back of the plane. Rhonda R. tells me to return to first class…I am more than happy to oblige! As I am returning to first class, I realize we have not taken off yet. Noticing that Captain Cecil S. II has stepped out of the cockpit, I try my best not to stare too hard. He comes closer to me as he makes his way across the cabin. He stops and takes in a whiff of my perfume. By now my heart is racing so fast that I have to take a deep breath again. *Pull yourself together, Janelle! Those first-class passengers need your undivided attention. It's no time to run back to the restroom.* Sitting in my seat, all I can think about is this good-looking young man. He looks to be in his late twenties, or early thirties. At this point, I decide to call Captain Cecil S. II, Superman. The name is fitting because he has wings and loves to fly. I wonder if he notices that I'm peeping his game! I can't stop blushing!

Next, Fernando Aka Dog goes over the safety video, telling the passengers that their seat cushions can be used for floating in water in an emergency. We also discussed putting the oxygen mask on themselves before they put it on an infant or small child.

Sean M. tells the flight attendants to do the crosscheck because we are number three in line for takeoff. Then, I ask all my passengers to look at the safety material, because all the instructions are located in the front seat pocket. The passengers need to know what to do in case of an emergency.

We take off and once we get over ten thousand feet, I start to serve my first-class passengers. I can't help but notice that this guy keeps staring at me. Next thing, I know he winks his eye at me. I just keep on working, making sure everyone gets a drink. As I am passing out drinks and snacks in first class, a man taps me on the shoulder to request a Coke and Patron. He says his name is Jay. This guy is beyond handsome with Armani eyeglasses, pretty brown eyes and full, juicy lips. It's obvious that I loved nice lips on a man. I wanted to lean over and kiss those lips nice and slow, enjoying the softness and warmth. I'm normally a one-man woman, but all this testosterone got me wanting both Superman and Jay! *Damn! Girl, do you realize, you're at work now?! Snap out of it!*

Jay lets me know he will be staying at The St. Regis Hotel in Houston.

"I'd love to have dinner with you tonight." His voice is deep and raspy. This guy wants dinner, but I want his chocolate body slathered with whipped cream! A girl can dream! While I'm giving Jay his Coke and Patron, he passes me his business card.

"I'm the CEO of a diamond and pearl store in Hawaii." Upgrade! Both Superman and Jay make bank!?

The guy who is sitting next to him introduces himself as Tavares and gives me his business card too. His card says he's the CEO of a private security company. Thanking them both, I let them know how nice it was to meet them. Then I return to collect empty glasses and trash. I'm having a great conversation with both guys.

"Are you Jay's bodyguard or something?" I ask Tavares.

Jay speaks up and answers instead. "Yes, he does excellent work. Why? Do you need someone to guard your beautiful body?"

That makes me blush and let out a flirtatious giggle. "You're silly."

"I'm serious. Be my date tonight?"

The word yes flies out of my mouth way too fast. Am I acting a little too thirsty? It might just be the hormones.

"Great. I'll have my driver pick you up. Just let me know where you'll be staying tonight."

A driver? For me? I love being treated like the queen I know I am!

When I walk away, he has the biggest smile on his face. Honestly, I am grinning from ear to ear too. Me and the other flight attendants start cleaning up all the trash as we make our descent into HOU, TX.

The captain's voice comes over the intercom and tells us we are going to be landing shortly. Rhonda R. keeps staring at me with her eyebrows raised. She is really getting on my nerves and I so want off this plane! Finally, the plane pulls up to the gate and the passengers are gathering their belongings from the overhead bins. Sauntering towards the restroom to flush my face with water, I see Rhonda R. walk off with the unaccompanied minor to the gate agent and then sign off for the day.

The captain is standing by the front door saying goodbye to all the passengers. It was a short flight. Thank God for no drama! As I am exiting the plane, I see Superman again.

"Have a great night," I throw over my shoulder.

"I'll have a great night if I can spend it with you!" He shot back.

Floored, I realize that today I'd gotten more play than I'd had in a long time! Two sexy and attractive men! All I can think about is getting to my hotel room, laying down and closing my eyes! I'm tired. As I am checking in, I hear someone call my name! Guess who?! It is Superman!!! The crew always stays at the same hotel. We start talking and walking towards the elevator. I push the button for the fifth floor.

Superman whispers lustfully, "I'm on five too!"

"What room?"

"505."

"Hey! I'm in 504!"

It must be fate! Or could this just be luck? All I can think about is laying in Superman's arms on a soft, king sized, pillow top bed.

I've been waiting to relax in a hot bubble bath all day and my feet are killing me! After saying goodnight to Superman once again, I'm off to my room. Once I'm inside, I rush to the bathroom to run my bath. As I'm lowering my tired body into the tub, there's a soft, rapid knock at the door. Who is this knocking at this hour? I'm ready to relax.

Getting out of the soothing water, I jump up, put on a white, terry cloth robe and head to the door. It is Superman, so I open it.

"Can I come in?" His handsome features look even better to me close up.

"Uh, I was in the middle of a bath, but okay." Trying not to make my attraction too obvious, I don't let on that I want him bad.

He steps inside my room and I close the door behind him

"Are there any good restaurants around here?"

"A few. There's a good Chinese spot two blocks up."

"Okay, cool! I'm going to grab a quick bite!"

"Okay, enjoy!"

"What's up with you? You look really tense?" His eyes are full of concern.

"Probably because of the flight and all that standing. My back feels a little achy."

"Looks like you can use a good massage".

"I do. I wonder if there's a spa in the hotel."

"I think I can handle that for you." His smoldering eyes capture mine in an intense stare.

With no fight left in me, I relent.
"Lay down on your stomach."
There's no way I can't oblige.

Superman starts with my shoulders, kneading the tension out of my muscles. All I can think about is how great it feels. He continues to rub his hands down my back. As he reaches the small of my back, he kisses me there. His lips are sooo soft, just like I imagined! I don't want to seem desperate. So, I ask him, "What are you doing?"

He says, "Just relax, I got this!" Then, the unexpected happens. He grabs each of my thighs and spread them apart. I'm sure you know what comes next. This man has me screaming and climbing the walls in no time.

"Ohhh...mmm... Superman..." Losing myself in ecstasy, I can't help but reveal the nickname I gave him in my fantasies. After he comes up for air, he kisses my *second set* of lips. He slurps and sucks me oh so good.

"Wow... that feels like heaven... ohhhh... damn..." Grinding and pushing my pelvis against his skillful tongue, I'm about to melt in his mouth.

His lips are so warm, so soft, so wet. By then, I am already dripping wet and it's time to slide into home plate. It's the best oral sex I've had in a long time. He is giving me goose bumps all over my body while grabbing me and holding me very tight. Taking one of my nipples into his mouth, he suckles like a hungry baby. Suddenly, he picks me up and leans me against the wall. Wrapping my legs around his waist, I suck on his neck softly. He moves before I can leave a passion mark. Closing my eyes, I can't hold it in.

"Damn...ahhh... oooohhhh..." The way I am moaning and clawing at his back, you'd think the man is killing me. I am surprised that nobody calls security.

"You tryna have me crazy over you ain't you?" He stares into my eyes before crushing my lips with his.

"That's the plan," I reply when he finally releases my lips.

As he grips my ass, he squeezes and massages.

"You feel so good…" His eyes are vulnerable as he stares into them intensely.

This man is touching those spots that have never been touched before in all forty-one of my years. I'm about to change my whole life for the D. It's like I want to climb the wall it feels so damn good. At one point in time I have to ask him to lift his body, so I can breathe a little.

"Superman…" Holding on to him, I close my eyes and let the riveting climax course over my body.

Like a drug, it's intoxicating.

It has been a wonderful evening, but I have a hot date later with Jay! So, now I'm trying to get him out of my room. Superman gets dressed and stares at me as he licks those sexy lips.

"Thank you for a great time. I'd love to have dinner with you sometime," he says winking at me as he heads out the door. He rocked my world! While I am lying down, I decide to call Jay. This man put out all the stops to get me! He REALLY put forth a lot of effort, which was more than what I am used to receiving.

"I've been waiting patiently for your call. Are we still on for tonight?" He sounds even sexier over the phone. My response is a happy-toned, "Yes!"

"I know the perfect spot. It's fancy and five-star for a five-star woman. Oh, there's also a hidden surprise in the limo for you." He lays it on thick.

"I can't wait!" Words can't express my excitement.

We hang up and my mind is reeling. I'd just had mind blowing sex with the pilot I'd been crushing on for months and now I am about to go out with a fine, successful entrepreneur. When had my luck gotten that good?

Let me jump in the shower… NOW! My hair, makeup… ALL of me must look flawless! I MUST say that I did the damn thang! The driver calls my cell about an hour later and to my surprise is already downstairs waiting for me! I will not keep a man waiting, so I grab my purse, put my lipstick on and start to walk out. At the last minute, I turn around and decide to change my panties. Why? I have a sexy pair of red panties with drawstrings on each side. If I decide to get me some more dick tonight, Jay will have *easy* access! When I get downstairs to the limousine, the driver is standing outside holding a little, blue box with a pink velvet ribbon. He hands it to me as my eyes glisten with anticipation. As I open the box, my eyes light up and my mouth drops. I cannot believe what I am seeing. This man bought me a diamond necklace with matching earrings. Wow! There is a note enclosed that reads, *Your beauty needs to shine…* There are further instructions for me to look to my left. When I glance to my left, there are a few dozen beautiful, yellow roses. The card with the roses read, *I want to put a smile on your face.*

By now, I'm sending a mass text to my closest girlfriends, telling them all about the gifts I'd received from a man I barely knew and that I'd just hooked up with a young pilot that I work with. He is hot, so I had to have him. I know that he's younger than me, but once I put my eyes on what I want, I have to have it. My girlfriends joke that I am a freak and be strolling the playground for men! I'll be that! I'm a real cougar!

Jay went out of his way to make the night special for me. I'm going to let him know how appreciative I am for such an amazing date! I can't wait to see him. Calling Jay to thank him for the wonderful gifts, it's nice to be treated like a lady! He has really gone out of his way for me. My eyes fall right on his handsomeness when I spot him standing outside when we pull up to the restaurant. It is so beautiful. The driver gets out, opens my door and walks me towards Jay. As soon as I get close to Jay, he grabs me and pulls me into to his firm body.

"I've been waiting for this *all* day!"

This wonderful man wined and dined me, but all I could think about was being under Superman again. If I could have for what I want, I'd have Superman here AND now! At that very moment, I get a text from him. He wants me to know he is thinking of me. Awww, how sweet! It blew my head up to know that he is thinking of me before bed! Goodnight, Superman!

Dinner is fantastic with Jay! I have steak and lobster and Jay has lobster and octopus. The appetizers and drinks are great. Actually, I'm having a really good time!

"Let's go back to my hotel room. We can have dessert and coffee," Jay suggests with a knowing look of lust in his eyes.

"I'll have to take a rain check. It's getting late and I have a wake-up call at nine am. The shuttle is going to pick me back up before I head to Atlanta."

"Well, I definitely want to see you again and would like for you to visit me in Hawaii."

"I'd love to visit."

His alluring eyes continue to penetrate mine. "Just let me know when and I'll send you a plane ticket. All you have to bring is yourself and some clothes!"

I want to finish my chocolate mousse, but Jay tells me to bring it with me. We head back to the limousine, laughing and talking. Before I know it, Jay has his hands inside my shirt. He begins kissing me passionately on the lips. My first thought is, I wish this was Superman. However, as he continues kissing me, it feels good, so I continue. He unhooks my bra and then begins to softly kiss on my breasts. By this point, my panties are positively wet. I want him to stop, but it feels so good. Jay must have thought I wanted more, because he continues by trying to pull down my panties. By now, I am getting frustrated.

"Stop. I'm not ready for that."

Backing up from me he says, "You are just sooo attractive. I could not help himself. Will you please accept my apology? I didn't mean to come on so strong."

I am so thankful that it's a short ride from the restaurant to the hotel. Once Jay apologized to me, I felt that he was truly sincere. He asks me if he could walk me up to my room. I nod my head in agreement. Once we are inside the lobby, Jay leans over and tries to kiss me again.

"Have a good night Jay."

This nutcase has the nerve to say, "Let me walk you up to your room."

Rushing off to the elevators, I don't even bother to respond. Once I am safely inside my room, I hurry up and peel off all my clothes before jumping in the shower to wash the smell of cologne off me! To bed I go after that!

Who is knocking at my door at this hour?

"Janelle, it's Cecil! Open up!"

Cecil? How did you forget to call the front office to do a wake-up call for seven o'clock AM in the morning?

"Janelle, you need to get dressed and eat breakfast," he urges. Jumping in and out of the shower, I have no time to do my hair, so I put it back in a ponytail. After putting my makeup on, I throw all my clothes in the suitcase and run out the door. As soon as I get downstairs, they are still serving continental breakfasts. Thank God, I was just in time. Stuffing my face real fast, I realize the shuttle will be there to pick us up in less than five minutes.

The flight goes great! It's awesome to work with the same people with no drama. It is always fun! I can't imagine working with another crew! We land in ATL, GA before I know it. After a long day, all I want to do is take a hot shower and go to bed. All the crew members get off the plane, then jump onto the shuttle. Once we get to the hotel, everyone gets their room number and keycard. Walking to my room, I am so happy, to be off work. Suddenly, my phone rings, so I pick it up to answer.

A deep voice asks, "What color panties do you have on? Red, white, blue?"

The whole time, I'm hoping it's NOT Jay! The man starts laughing.

"Who is this?"

"You don't recognize my voice?"

"No, and you better tell me who you are before I give you the click!"

"Chill, baby! It's Cecil S. Uhhh…Superman!"

Oh! The one and only Superman! Slipping and calling him that in the midst of passion hadn't gone unnoticed.

"I like that name boo. Turns out we're next-door neighbors again!"

"How is that possible?"

Superman tells me, "Go to your door and open it."

True enough, there he is, all six feet of caramel deliciousness! Our rooms are across from each other again.

"Superman, who in scheduling are you paying?"

He chuckles and it turns me on.

"Would you like to come to my room tonight?" He reminds me that last time, we ended up in my room.

"Let's have dinner.

"Okay, that sounds perfect," he agrees.

The butterflies are stirring and I am getting antsy! What should I wear? Something sexy, or conservative? Again, I'm not desperate, even though in the back of my mind, I want to sleep with him again! So, for now, I'll play it cool! Looking in the mirror to make sure my hair looks nice and my makeup is flawless, I'm ready! I decide to wear a black strapless dress with a see-through back.

We take an Uber and have dinner at *Rays on the River* in Buckhead on the patio because it was such a nice warm, summer evening. He is already waiting for me at the table. As I walk toward him, Superman stands up and hands me a single-stem pink rose with a light kiss on my neck. He is smelling so good. All I can think about is finishing dinner and getting back to where we left off.

Superman asks, "What are your plans for the rest of the evening."

"Hopefully you!" My voice is seductive.

He flashes a sexy smile my way. "I can handle that!"

We are already in Buckhead so we get a suite at The Westin being that we don't want the crew to know we were doing the nasty. And this time, we have one room. As he begins to take off his clothes, I get the chance to see how sexy his body really is!

"How about I give you a massage, since you're undressed," I suggest.

"Okay," he decides to let me.

"Lay on the bed," I instruct.

After I pick up a small bottle of almond oil from the restroom, I begin to rub his back down. When I am finished, I ask him to turn over. Then I rub him down from the top of his head all the way down to where the volcano erupts. I am about to stop, but decide to keep going. He needs to feel what I felt the *first* time. All he can do is lay there and moan. Damn! I got him right where I want him!

We end up on the floor that time instead of in the bed. I'm putting it on him, so he starts to get a little tired. The reason I can tell is because he slows down his grind.

"You alright, Superman? You are *only thirty-three* years old…need I remind you?"

"How old are you, sexy lady?"

"Well, I'm just a *wee* forty-one years old and I'm aging gracefully!" Superman's eyes light up in surprise!

"No way! It's amazing how you can keep up with me…wow!"

Lying in his arms, I feel like a porcelain piece; delicate and treasured. Touching his arm, I softly whisper in his ear "Did you do a wake-up call for the morning shuttle?"

"Go back to sleep. I've got everything under control."

After a short nap we go back to the other hotel.

At seven in the morning the alarm clock goes off just as my phone starts ringing. Realizing that Superman is not in the bed with me, I sit at the edge of the bed and answer the phone.

"Good morning, boo! How did you sleep?"

Immediately recognizing that silky smooth voice, I reply,

"I slept just like a baby! If only you could see this big smile on my face." My legs are shaking as I melt to the sound of his voice.

"Sorry, but I can't talk long. I have to jump in the shower."

"I'd pay to see that sexy body again!"

"I will see you downstairs shortly." We don't have long before we have to be at the shuttle.

Finally, we make it to the shuttle with all the crew ready for the flight from ATL back to MIA. So relieved that it's a short flight, I cannot wait to get home! After we return to MIA, all the crew start gathering their luggage. I just happen to be up front and Superman is a few feet ahead of me. He starts flicking his tongue at me, while I roll my eyes. Then, he jumps in front of me and begins gyrating his hips seductively as we are walking off the plane. My eyes are glued to his round, plump butt. His moves are cute, yet tastefully inviting. He has me sprung!

"Now remember, we have to act professionally when we are out in public."

"Are you going home just yet?" Superman questions.

"No, I was just going to run a few errands first."

"I'd like to come over."

"Come over and do what?"

"I'll make it worth your while…I always do!"

"Alright! I'll text you my address"

Tonight, is the night that I become Superwoman. The way I am feeling, we are going half on a baby. I look through my bag for my Victoria's Secret black push-up bra and panty set. Superman calls to let me know that he is ten minutes away. I let him know that the door is open and to just come in. It is obvious that I am anxious, because I am pacing back and forth. About ten minutes later, I hear my security alarm alerting that the front door has opened.

"Superman is that you?" I call out.

"Yes, it's me, Janelle!"

"Come upstairs to the bedroom!"

Superman's eyes bulge when he sees me looking all hot in my lingerie. Laying on the bed in a sexy pose, I'm trying to look more than cute.

"Mmm, you're so sexy!" He bites down on his bottom lip as he stares me down.

"The shower's running.

Follow me to the bathroom."

He does and we begin to undress. He lets his blue boxers fall to the floor as I quickly remove my bra and panties.

"Hold up. Just stand there for a minute and let me admire your body."

So, I do!

This man is really turned on by my body and that turns me on. We get in the shower and he starts kissing and nibbling on my neck.

"Ohhh, Superman. That feels so good." Things are starting to get really hot and steamy, so we decide to get out.

He picks me up and places me on the bed. The whole time my body feels like putty in his arms. This man has me so gone. He reaches over my head, and I think he is getting a condom, but I am wrong.

"I wanna feel you... skin to skin," he whispers seductively.

For some reason, I didn't oppose to that.

Stroke after stroke, he give me what I want, exactly *how* I want it.

"Janelle, mmm... you know you're the best, right?" As he asks, he's gently sucking on my earlobe.

"Uhhh... yesss... right there, Superman, don't stop..."

Holding on to his thick butt cheeks, I let him take me on yet another orgasmic trip to the cosmos and back again.

Before I can finish washing off in the bathroom, he bends me over the sink and we start going at it again. That time I have multiple orgasms and actually start squirting. The sight really turns him on and he really goes in.

"Ohhh myyy…" He's so deep inside me, it's like I feel him in my chest.

Honestly, I like it rough.

I am super exhausted after round two. Damn! I didn't know that being with a young thang would have me wide open like this. I need a break!!!

So, I lay comfortably in his strong arms and drift off to sleep. Oh, what a magical night! Superman…this man has me wide open. I've never been with someone like him, especially as young as he is. This might be a new and exciting journey for me! He just might be my new boo. We are so compatible. To make the time with him last forever would be a dream come true.

"Can you drop me off to get my car keys from a friend? I took an Uber here," Superman says.

We start making small talk and I ask him, "So, who is this *mystery* friend"

"She's an RN in the Ob/Gyn. She works at Mercy Hospital. That's where I need to go," he goes on to explain.

"Are you for real? My sister, Lisa works at the same hospital! She is an OB/GYN with a specialty in high risk pregnancies."

"That's the same department my friend works in!"

"Wouldn't it be funny if they know each other?"

Superman starts to grimace.

"No, Janelle! It would not."

"Who is she to you? Mother? Sister? Roommate?"

Superman began to play with his tie as if he's nervous.

"No…she's my fiancée"

"Did you say fiancée?"

"Yes, Janelle! She's *my* fiancée! What is it to you?" Suddenly his eyes are dark and empty.

By now, I'm thinking to myself, this man just played me! He made passionate love to me and he's booed up! At this point in my forty-one years of life, I couldn't care less about a fiancée? I'm a real cougar! Doesn't this young man know that he has been captured by a wise woman? If he can keep up with me, I'm going to teach him some more lessons. Then reality sets in and I know what I have to do. Superman reaches over to hug me, but I extend my hand instead.

On the way to the hospital, I don't say anything to him. I'm so in shock that he didn't tell me that from the beginning. After I drop him off at the hospital, I speed off screeching tires! A river of tears runs down my cheeks, as I drive away.

As soon as I get home, I throw all my stuff in the middle of the floor and go upstairs to run me a bubble bath. It's so hard to believe what a horrible day I've had! Superman thinks because he's charming and good-looking that he can pull a fast one on me. We'll see who has the last laugh! The more I think about it, the more pissed off I feel. If I ever – EVER see that man again, I will have a few choice words for him! He *really* played me! A player got played!

Two months went by and I hadn't heard anything from Superman. My routine returns to all work and no play. Then a wave of nausea hits me like a ton of bricks! Before I can throw up all over myself, I tell the other flight attendant that I need to go to the restroom. As soon as I close the door, my head is in the toilet calling Earl. It feels like it will never stop. Was it something I ate? I couldn't remember, so I let it go and return to work. Maybe if I drink some ginger ale, I'll feel better. I try to drink more towards the end of the shift, but it doesn't help. There is a stomach virus going around and maybe I have caught it. I'll call my sister Lisa in the morning. I'm going to leave her a message now, so I can see her asap since she's a doctor.

Lisa calls me the next morning and tells me to come in around five pm, since that's when it slows down in her office. When I arrive at the hospital, I don't think it's anything major. Lisa tells me to have a seat so she can do blood work on me. Easy breezy. But the longer I sit there, I begin to think something is really wrong. Lisa walks back into the room.

"Girl, what have you been doing?"

"Nothing! Just traveling and hooking up with my new bae! Well, he was my new bae."

"Your new bae? What do you mean?"

"You know! The one who was breaking my back nice and good."

"Well, you're running a slight temperature."

"Really! What is causing it?"

"The lab results from your blood work will be back soon. Hold on!"

My sister leaves and about fifteen minutes later walks back in the room. I've never seen that expression on her face before.

"Stella, while you were getting your groove back, did you use a condom?

"Yeah, a couple of times, but that third time, we went all out and didn't use one! Why'd you ask?"

"Because your test results came back and you're pregnant. My sister?" That heifer is looking all gleeful, but my expression doesn't match hers."

"How is that possible? I'm forty-one years old!"

"Uhhh…we know *how* you got pregnant!"

Covering my face with my hands, I cry. "Lord, what am I going to do now? How can I tell Superman that he is going to be a father? I haven't thought about him lately. I've been so busy with work. But, the real question is, am I ready to be a mother? Will I blow up like a balloon? Superman told me he has a fiancée and he's getting married. Married? He never even mentioned to me that he had a girlfriend!"

"You still need to tell him," my sister says, rubbing my back soothingly.

"It's too complicated sis. I don't want to talk about it right now." By now my sister is starting to get pissed off. "So, this guy can drop a load on you and still get married? Go home and get some rest and I'll call you in the morning."

As I am driving home, my brother Teddy calls.

"Sis, how are you doing?"

"Not too good, but I'm good and pregnant!"

"Good and pregnant with what? Expectation?"

"Nah! You're going to be an uncle. It's still new. I don't even know the sex yet."

"Who's the baby daddy? There is a baby daddy."

"It's the captain I told you about, so he ain't broke!"

"Well at least you'll have diapers, wipes and formula on the regular!"

"He has a fiancée and I didn't know it."

"I'm sure that wedding will be officially off! Call me back when you get yourself together sis."

"I'll do what is necessary, Teddy…or die trying!"

Needing some time to myself to think, I ponder how I am going to handle this situation? Looking at Superman's number, I'm wondering if I should call him, or not. That's when I take a deep breath and dial it. He picks up right away.

"I've been trying to call you. I'm sure you heard the news. I'm getting married really soon."

"Married? So, you really are gonna go through with it? You didn't even tell me anything about her before you slept with me. What about what we had?"

"Yes, Janelle! We had a good time together, but it was just sex!"

Those words knock the air out of me, but I must let him know. "Well, the news I have to tell you is a result of that."

"Result of what? What are you saying?"

"I'm pregnant, Superman! You're gonna be a father!"

Suddenly the tone of his voice changes. He sounds extremely angry. "Well, it ain't mine!"

"How can you say that?"

"You gave it up to me so easy. I don't know how many other men you slept with!"

"Do the math for yourself. The doctor confirmed it. I'm two months pregnant. Like it or not, he or she is coming!"

"You're not going to mess up my plans. I've got one hundred people coming to the wedding. It's going off without a hitch."

I am devastated by his response.

"Who is a *baby mama* at forty-one anyone!" With that said, he hangs up.

Promising myself that I never want to see him again from that day on, I know it is just going to be me and my baby.

Two weeks have gone by and I am on my way home from a trip. My cell phone rings and on the other end is an unfamiliar man's voice.

"How are you doing, Ms. Love?"

"Who is this?"

"This is Tavares. You met me on a flight two months ago, remember?"

He starts to refresh my memory. He owns a security company and he does security for Mr. Jay.

"Yes, I remember you? What made you call me?"

"I have something really messed up to tell."

I am laying down, but I sit up to listen to his news. He goes on to refer to Superman's real name.

"Uh, yeah, I'm very familiar with him."

"Well, I met him after that flight and gave him my card. He contacted me and he wants me to kill you!"

"Kill me?"

By now, I'm shaking uncontrollably and all kinds of crazy thoughts are running through my head.

"Why would he want to have me killed?"

"He said he just got news that you are pregnant by him. He feels that you are going to ruin his future. He is getting married…and if his fiancée finds out, he will lose the love of his life."

"What did you tell him?"

"Told him I will get back to him in about a week. You got a few days to figure out what to do. I'm just calling you to give you a heads up! This guy's not playing. Your life is in danger."

"What will I do?"

"Well, I'm not gonna do the job… of course. You don't deserve that. Just be careful, because I'm sure that he'll go to someone else to do the job.

"Tavares, thank you so much for calling me."

Immediately, I get off the phone to start packing my clothes. Panic is starting to set in and my next thought is, where was I going to go? My next move is to call my mother and father to them that they are going to be grandparents.

"Hi ma, is daddy near you?"

"Yes, he's right here."

"Okay. Well, I am calling to tell you that you are going to be grandparents."

"Oh, my baby, that's so exciting." She has me on speaker phone so I hear my pops loud and clear.

"Congrats baby girl!"

"I'm leavin' the country. I'm going to spend some time with Teddy," I say.

"But why are you leaving the country after you told us such exciting news."

Letting out a deep breath, I go on to explain. "My baby's daddy put a contract out for someone to kill me because I am pregnant. I don't feel safe, so I think it's best for me to leave."

"Oh my, you must call the police and report him!" My mother exclaimed.

"Nah, you need to let me get my hands on that piece of…"

Cutting my pops off, I say, "I'll handle it daddy. I don't want you doing anything to get locked up for."

After ending the call with them, I call my job to let them know that I am resigning for emergency reasons. I ask them to send all my important paperwork to my parents' house and gave them the forwarding address. Then, I call my sister Latoya, my attorney, to tell her I received a disturbing call.

"My baby's daddy put a contract out for someone to kill me because I am pregnant," I explain.

"Are you kidding me?" Her voice is full of concern.

"No, sis it's true. Can you come pick me up and take me the airport. I'm leaving the country. I'm going to stay with Teddy. Tell my real estate agent that he can sell my house." I'll miss sunny Miami; my true home!

"Sis, I'll be on my way in about thirty minutes. Hold tight. Oh my gosh!"

My sister must be a true speed demon because she is knocking on my door within twenty-two minutes flat. She gets me to the airport on time. My international flight to Germany is scheduled to leave in two hours.

I'm so happy that I'm leaving and I was warned in time. I feel so much safer at the airport. Even if I ran into the captain, who had put a hit out on me, he couldn't do anything to me. I hug my sister and after what feels like the longest walk in the world, I finally board the plane. The plane finally takes off and I have a long flight ahead. My brother Teddy is there at the airport to pick me up. He is so happy to see me. I live with my brother for a few months and then buy my own home after they sell my house in the states. Seven months later, I give birth to a little boy, never to once think about Superman again.

MASK OF DECEPTION

Have you ever been to a masquerade party? The essence of intrigue, mystery and anonymity excites me! Never have I been to one, but I've heard all about them. My best friend, Ms. Chanel Candy invited me to her masquerade party. This chick woke me up at about nine in the morning raving about the menu and all the eligible bachelors that would be there. Chanel has been working for eight months on closing a business deal, which is her biggest project yet. She is glad the worst is over and wants to just chillax and party.

One of her investors is a rich business man named, Mr. Luca Sullo aka Small. He's quiet and shy, but his bank account made a lot of noise. His money was long and his pockets were deep. "Mr. Money Bags" gave Chanel almost a quarter of a million dollars. All her family and friends are flying into Memphis, Tennessee. The planning of this event starts to get next to her and she begins pacing the floor. Sweat is visible on her brow.

"Tasha, you're coming through, right?! I need you by my side!" She pleads.

"You're my best friend! Besides, If I don't show up, you might stop speaking to me."
That's when she burst out into hysterical laughter. "Yeah, true! I need you, girl! I need you like rice needs gravy!"

"Rice needs gravy? Now, that's corny." Not able to help it, I let out a chuckle myself.

"Thank you for being a true friend, Chanel!"

"I love you, Tasha!"

"I love you more," is my affectionate response.

Chanel lets me know that her schedule is busy for the evening, but her morning is free. She told me that she will open the boutique at 6pm for VIP and 7pm to the general public. Everyone in Memphis will be able to shop and check out her new boutique. Chanel has always loved shoes, hence the reason she's opening a shoe boutique.

That's when she blurted out excitedly, "It's going to be called *Chanel Stepping Out.*"

"Why did you name it that?" Liking the name, I was just curious.

"Because ladies will be stepping out for the evening in their pumps! It's going to be in downtown Memphis in the district area, not far from the Mississippi River."

"Chanel, that name is very catchy! You go girl! Get that money!"

"Thank you, girl!"

Chanel's boutique will have all name brand shoes and they won't be any knock-offs, or made with fake leather. She further described that the shoes will all be four-inch heels with a genuine leather lining as well as her personal signature, which is the initials C.S.O. (Chanel Stepping Out).

"Memphis today and international tomorrow," I confidently declare.

"Yes, ma'am!" Chanel agrees.

Slowly starting to wake up, I clear my throat, sounding like a frog.

"Memphis has some powerful business women. I must give you kudos, Chanel! What a great marketing strategy. Putting your company's name and initials inside the shoes…that way, everybody will know they came from *your* boutique."

Chanel goes on to explain that all her favorite colors; red, black and blue, will always be in stock. She let me know that all her shipments of quality, designer pumps will be imported from Rome, Italy. To say that I was impressed was to say the least.

Suddenly, there is dead silence. Is there something wrong with my phone?

"Tasha are you still there?"

"Yes, I'm here. My phone's just acting up."

Chanel begins to pick back up where she left off. "Prices will start at eighty five dollars and range up to a thousand!"

There's no way she had it like that! What a nice profit margin! "Chanel be quiet and take a deep breath. You just keep talking!"

"I was born for this, Tasha!"

"Can we change the subject for a minute?" My sly side wants to come out.

"Sure, Tasha! What is it?" She sounds disappointed.

"Will I get a chance to meet Mr. Luca Sullo…the man from Italy? He sounds very intriguing. Especially being that he's from Italy! I've never met anyone from Rome, Italy!"

"Well, he's been in town for six weeks and will be returning to Italy tomorrow. He's not only helping me with my business, but he has other obligations." Chanel is talking so fast, I can barely keep up. Where's an iced coffee when you need it? A caffeine fix is what I need, and like now!

"Do you realize it's only nine on a Saturday morning and it's my day off!"

Sucking her teeth, she jokes, "Girl, so you lost some sleep! So, what! Ain't like I pulled you away from a bae!"

"Did you forget the rule to never ever, ever, ever call me before ten am?"

"Tasha, get your butt up and let's go to brunch."

That heifer still isn't taking me seriously. Against my will, I figure I may as well just give up on sleep.

"Okay, but if I get up, I get to choose the restaurant."

"Whatever you want, ma'am!" Chanel agrees good-naturedly.

"Chanel, girl when you get to this restaurant, you are going to enjoy their soul food!"

"It better be finger licking good!"

"You better believe it is! It's about to go *down*, girl! *Southern Hands Home-Style Cooking* is on the eastside. We may run into some traffic, but the food is worth it! They serve lunch from 11am until 2 pm. I discovered this little wonder of the world on my way out of town, on a flight from Memphis to Jacksonville via Atlanta. I remember it vividly, because it was during the holidays when I was visiting relatives."

"It must be hard not having your mother and father for the holidays." Chanel is clearly getting choked up. "They are looking down on you from heaven."

"I don't know what I would do if I didn't have a friend like you, Chanel. Thank you!"

"Finish telling me the rest of the story," Chanel says anxiously.

"So, I met one of the owners connecting, from gate-to-gate at the airport. She and her significant other were on their way to a seminar coming from Memphis like me. She informed me that she has a family business here and invited me to lunch. We exchanged numbers. She told me to call her before I arrive and I could even bring a friend or two. Lunch is on her!"

"Tasha, can I bring my last two living aunties?" Chanel begged.

Smacking my lips, I say, "You always want your aunties to go everywhere with you."

"They are my favorite women in the whole wide world," she declares.

"It's not a party... You can't have your whole family coming." We both start to chuckle a little.

"Your aunts...I understand they're old and everything, but their ears can't tolerate anything X-rated!" I squeal.

"I'm so excited and can't wait to see this restaurant, Tasha!"

"You're going to love it."

"For the last time, did you get your butt out of the bed girl?" Chanel acts like she's my mama...always reminding me of what to do and when to do it. "Oh, and hold up! Hold up! Don't forget to take your medication! When you miss your meds, your split personality, Tess comes out with guns blazing! She's a true evil diva...always lit! Haaa!"

"I stay all the way turnt up! You didn't know hoe!"

"So, who's a hoe now? I don't be out there like that, but all this ain't free. Have you heard? You got to pay to play!"

"Hoe!" Tasha squeals jokingly.

The both of us can't help but laugh.

"Seriously though, the last time you forgot to take your meds, we got into a big fight and I had to drop your tail off at the psych ward. Promise me you won't mess up my special day! Do you hear me Tasha?"

I'm a twilight zone mess.com with two sides. One is good and the other is pure evil!

"Girl, get off the phone! I'll see you soon," I tell her before shaking my head.

The night before, I fell asleep on the couch. My back is stiff as a board when I wake up. Getting up slowly, I go to rub some *Icy Hot* on it. After that, I run upstairs and jump in the shower. Once I'm all squeaky clean, I do my hair and makeup. The goal to look fleekish had been accomplished. Satisfied with my look, I pack a suitcase for later that night, knowing that I won't have enough time to come back home. After all the rushing and trying to get ready, I grab three outfits for Chanel's grand opening. Running out the door, I forget to take my medication. What's going on with my brain today? Remembering to text Chanel the address of the restaurant while I am sitting in the driveway, I wait for her to respond. She lets me know that she is on her way. Pulling off in my fully loaded Lexus truck with tinted windows, I take in the scenic route.

When I'm halfway to the restaurant, I am stopped by a red light. Rolling down my window, I see a really good-looking guy parked right next to me. Proceeding to honk my horn, I can't help but admire his red convertible. Red is my color! He looks at me and that's when I motion for him to roll down his window.

"Hey pretty lady! How are you?" There is a broad smile on his mocha toned face.

"Fine, but I'm going to need you to pull over!" By now, my second personality Tess, the personality that Chanel never likes, comes out to play. His eyes light up. This man looks puzzled and confused, probably wondering if I'm a po-po. But the funny thing about it is, he does exactly what I told him to do. We both pull into a gas station parking lot and get out of our cars simultaneously.

"Are you a cop, or something?" His sexy eyes cast down on me.

"No, you're so good-looking, so I had to pull you over." I'm trying to entice him with my voluptuous curves.

"Well, I've never had a woman pull me over before."

He starts laughing and so do I.

"That's kind of sexy though. You see what you want and you go after it. What's your name?"

"Tess," She catches herself. "I'm Tasha and you are?"

"Chase."

That's when I start laughing to myself. Isn't that ironic? I'm really trying to chase him. That is too funny.

Deciding to ask if we can exchange numbers, I wonder how his deep voice sounds over the phone.

"What's the rush pretty lady?" Chase questions.

"My sister and I have a lunch date," I simply say.

He nods and pulls out his wallet. "Here's my business card. Call me anytime." We are standing so close.

He is checking me out, while I peep his nice ass.

"You are gorgeous! Mmm! You're wearin' them jeans too. They showin', all those delicious curves." He is even bolder than I am. Wow.

Deciding to speak my mind too, I say, "Chase, the sight of your juicy lips is making me hot. I can't even lie."

That's when my phone rings. It is Chanel wondering where I am.

"Girl, I'm in the restaurant parking lot." With my eyes on Chase, I quickly end the call. Chase starts being nosey and is all up in my business.

"Where is your sister and is she as cute as you?"

Trying to play it off like, I act as if I didn't hear him. I fake a coughing attack. "Um excuse me…got a little frog in my throat!" Inwardly, I am laughing *hard*!

"Can I call you on Sunday? Is that a good time for you baby girl? "Yes, you can you call me after three, I'll just be getting home from

church and need to wind down a little. Is that ok with you, Chase?!

"Yes, baby girl. I'm looking forward to talking with you on Sunday." That's when he grabs my arm and pulls me closer to him, giving me a tight hug. Oh my gosh! This guy has me melting. His arms are so strong. I'm starting to get hot and it isn't due to the weather!

It is a hot summer day of about ninety degrees. He has on a Polo shorts set. Everything he has on is Polo, down to his socks. Chase has this wonderful smelling cologne on that is making my head swim. He is 5'10, with an almond toned complexion and an athletic build. Not able to help it, I grab his butt and start squeezing him. We both are enjoying each other, but this is not like me.

That's when a familiar voice kicks in. "It's not you, it's me Tessa!" Oh crap! I did forget to take my medication. There's no time to turn around and go home to get it. Chanel is waiting on me. I'm just going to have to play it calm and collective and pray she doesn't catch on.

By now, it's clear that I'm not in control of myself. It is all Tess!

"Gotta go Chase! Talk to you later."

"Did I do something wrong?" He looks so hurt.

"No, everything's cool. Let's talk on Sunday." Jumping in my car, I pull off. Once I am back in my vehicle, I look in my rearview mirror and notice Chase is still standing there. Tess, don't mess up this day. Desperately trying to get back to normal self, I realize that I can't let Chanel see Tess. "Lord, let me just be able to make it through this day."

Finally reaching the restaurant, I pull up next to Chanel's car. She jumps out as soon as she sees me.

"You told me you were already here. I've been waiting on you for like ten minutes."

Ignoring her annoyance, I say, "Well, I'm ready to eat, are you? Let's go in!" I snap.

As we walk in closer to the bar, the food has such a wonderful aroma. You can smell the delicious scents of candied yams, collard greens and homemade macaroni and cheese. We both turn to each-other

"It's about to go down!" We say in unison.

That's when Chanel asks me, "Did you take your medication? You know you *must* take it before you eat."

"Yes, ma'am." As I salute her, she doesn't know I am telling a bold-faced lie. One of the owners comes out and greets us with a bright smile. She shows us to our table, near the patio. The ambiance is wonderful.

"Hello, ladies, how are you?" She asks.

"We're doing great and you? Last time we saw each other, we were passing through the airport."

"Yeah, that was an extremely hectic day. I almost left my carry-on bag in the restroom."

"My name is Tess and this is my good friend Chanel."

Chanel slightly turns to her left and says, "Do you realize what you just said?"

"I'm just playing, girl. You know it's me, Tasha."

Chanel grabs me by the arm, staring me down like I stole something. "Stop playing like that. We have no time for Tess."

One of the owners of the restaurant volunteers to give us a tour.

"Tasha, let me show you two around. Here's the kitchen. I remodeled it myself!" She sounds pretty enthusiastic.

The owner looks at us and explains, "I have to get back to work. You ladies enjoy your meal and don't forget it's on me."

Our server approaches the table and Chanel asks, "Do ya'll serve chitterlings?"

Not able to hold in my laugh, I must be honest. Those things stink.

"Oh! Okay. You gon' have chitlin' breath!" I tease.

"Tasha, just add some hot sauce on 'em and I'm happy!" She defends her taste.

"Collard greens, macaroni and cheese and fried chicken sounds good to me, Chanel."

"I've never seen you eat fried chicken before. You so bougie. You won't even eat the skin!"

"Well, I got a taste for it now. Drown them wangs in honey and hot sauce…I'm gon' be lit!"

"That doesn't sound like you. Are you okay?" Her eyes are on me in concern.

"Just trying something new. What's with the food interrogation?" We order our food and then the server brings us our drinks. As we sip, we continue our conversation about our day. When the food comes, we are amazed at the large portion sizes. Chanel and I swallow our food down like two fat pigs. Ready for dessert, Chanel and I share a bowl of peach cobbler with a side of vanilla ice cream. Our bellies are full and it is time to go.

"Are we stopping by your office or going to the boutique?" I ask Chanel.

"I need to stop by the office to confirm details with my assistant Kevin."

Deciding to follow her, I figure I can get dressed at her office. Chanel suggests we go the boutique because there is more room.

That's when her cell phone rings. She answers and I can faintly hear someone screaming on the other end.

"Sis, where are you? How close are you to the airport? I'm just leaving my office. What's up!"

She goes on to explain that she hired a limousine service to pick them up and drop them off at the boutique. "It's 4:30 PM. I'm really irritated and don't like it when things don't go my way!" Her sister rants.

"I'm so excited that you guys are here! My sisters, my hittas!" Chanel says.

"You gon' feed us? First class didn't give us *big* girls much. Do they think we're on diets?" One of them ask playfully

"Y'all want some soul food?" Chanel asks.

Rolling my eyes, I think to myself, 'Hell nah! They'll eat the place out of business!'

Chanel starts laughing. "My sisters are too funny. All they think about is food, sun up to sun down! It's not healthy to be that big."

Side eying her, I say, "Oh, girl leave them alone! Everyone can't be a toothpick like you, Chanel."

After that I follow her to her office.

We pick up her laptop and some other boxes before loading up the car. As we are walking toward the door, she asks her assistant if Mr. Luca had called. Kevin informs her that Mr. Luca is in route to the boutique. She snaps on him.

"Why didn't you tell me that he called? What am I paying you for? If I have to remind you of one thing, you'll be applying for jobs on Indeed.com faster than you can say *unemployed!*" She is fired up!" Kevin points to his text messages, showing her his outbox.

"Chanel, you be doing the most. You see it now?" He abruptly turns around and walks away.

"My bad, Kevin! You're right...I did see that. I just forgot." Chanel be going off on folks. I wouldn't want to get on her bad side.

"We need to leave right now! Let's go, Chanel!" She is not going to mess up my day with that stank attitude. If I read her, she's going to try me and get these hands! Don't try Tess! We have a short thirty-minute drive back to the boutique. Her employees had set up everything and it is looking nice. There is a live band, ice sculptures and a life-size stiletto fashioned into a photo booth. The ambiance is on fleek, so Tasha and I need to get dressed quickly. As we are putting on foundation, the MC announces that Chanel's family has arrived.

When Chanel's sisters see her, they sandwich her in like an Oreo cookie. She introduces them to me. They pay me compliments on my makeup, eyelashes and eyebrows. My makeup is always on fleek. I can't help but take in all this Tasha love. Chanel starts to get worried because she doesn't see her mother.

"Where's mama?"

"Mom drank a lot of water. You know she's seventy years old and stays glued to the toilet," one of her sisters point out.

That's when the door opens. In walks a short woman of about 4'11 with sandy-brown hair, hazel eyes and large hips. Her confidence lingers in the air. I want to be like her when I grow up. Get it mama!

"How's my little girl doing?" Chanel's mom beckons her for a hug. Chanel tries to hide her embarrassment. Even Stevie Wonder can see she loves her mama.

"I'm not your little girl anymore ma."

"You'll always be my little girl." She starts to take a trip down memory lane, looking off into the distance. "I remember when you sang, 'Saving All My Love' in the *Little Miss Memphis* pageant. Everyone was clapping and hollering 'sing, baby!' Now, *my* baby is all grown up!"

"Mama, enough with this family reunion! Go grab your mask and get dressed. I have a very important client waiting on me. Time is money, for real!"

"You don't have to be so bossy, Chanel!" Her mom retorts with a frown.

"I'm so sorry, mama. I just have a lot to do."

She grabs the contract and out the door we go. As soon as we walk out, everyone is donning their masks. A fine, sexy man with a gray suit and red handkerchief in his top right pocket, is standing in the corner talking on a cell phone. Chanel recognizes him *immediately* as the one and only Mr. Luca Sullo. She decides to walk up to him and spit some small talk.

"Good evening, Mr. Luca!" She shakes his hand.

"Ms. Chanel Candy! You look stunning. Love your mask by the way!"

"Yours is very intriguing! Where did you get it?"

"I had it shipped from Italy. So, you like my style?"

The chemistry between them is undeniable. This coupling needs a monkey wrench and who better than the sexy and more confident Tess. Tapping Chanel on the shoulder, I'm giving her a sideways stank face. She gives me a sneer!

"So, you're not going to introduce us?" This chick thinks she slick. I'll show her.

"Sure. Mr. Luca, this is my best friend, Tasha."

Seeing that Mr. Luca's staring me up and down, I can tell he's feeling me.

"Lovely mask. May I have this dance?"

"Of course," I oblige.

As he walks me to the dance floor, I ask him, "Do you like to kiss?"

He mumbles, "What type of kiss?"

What? This man needs coaching. We dance to four songs back to back. He might not know much about kissing, but he is a wonderful dancer! Pulling the multi-millionaire in closer to my body, he smells so good. Noticing that the music stops abruptly, we end our dance.

Chanel starts to give her speech. She thanks everyone for coming and invites them to check out her boutique's shoe collection. She must've spied all the money in the room. That Chanel is a mess. She tells the husbands of her female guests, "Open those fat wallets for the lady in your life!"

The room fills with laughter.

Everything is going so perfectly. Chanel is so happy to see her family and friends. I can't help but admire a tall, handsome specimen standing in the corner by himself. As I try to catch his eye, he doesn't seem to notice. Next thing I know, a lady is tapping me on my shoulder trying to get my attention.

"Stay outta my man's face before I bust your head to the white meat!" She's all in my grill and her breath is tart.

"Whatever, lady! Don't want your man! He ain't my type. He probably doesn't want you with that stank breath." I am sure she's talking about the fine dark brother I was just eyeing.

Then the chick punched me in my face. What the hell? It's about to go down! With one swift motion, I throw an uppercut, punching her in the chin. Suddenly someone comes over and breaks us up. Chanel is looking at me like I'm crazy? You think I'm about to let someone touch me and they not catch these hands? Chanel casually walks over to us. "What's going on?"

"Are you serious, Chanel?! This chick gon' make me mop the floor with her messed up ass weave."

Chanel steps between us and pulls me to the side, while the other chick is removing her stilettos and hoops. Tess is visibly lit and ready to throw down. I will not be disrespected...EVER!

"You gon' learn today!"

Ready to chin check that chick again, Chanel gets in my face. I can tell she is hot by her facial expression.

"Y'all not 'bout to come in here with all this bs. If y'all don't leave now! I'm gettin' ready to shut the both of y'all down! Comin' up in my party actin' like a bunch of hoodrats! I can't believe you'd do this to me Tasha!"

And then she begins to cry real tears. She is just a boo-hooing! Touching her on the shoulder, I know I have to apologize. "My bad! I'm sorry! I can get a little crazy when I don't take my meds. I'll see myself out. I'm leaving now."

Tess is so messy. She makes Tasha seem so ratchet.

Chanel

With Tasha gone and me being *the* finest woman here, I get to have Mr. Luca all to myself!

Two hours have passed by and Mr. Luca has yet to even ask me for a dance. I'll just go ask him and beat him to the punch. When I walk over to the mirror to adjust my hair, there Mr. Luca is standing next to me.

"I need to leave shortly because I have an early am flight. Chanel, do you have the contract?"

"Yes, we can step into my office for some privacy." So, we step off and take the elevator to the 2nd floor. Inside the tight quarters of the elevator, I can't help but be drunk by the intoxicating scent of his *Gucci Guilty Black*. He's Italian. We would look good together and have some beautiful babies. Beginning to imagine us having phone sex, and him spittin' that Italian *facciamo l'amore* (make love to me), I can feel my panties moisten. They are literally sticking to me. As we turn the corner and walk the short corridor to my office, Mr. Luca begins to admire the vaulted ceilings and picturesque view of downtown Memphis. His eyes are steadfastly glued to the purple leather sofa in the center of the room.

"Can we sit? The décor in your office is very beautiful! Nothing like my dull and boring office."

SHE'LL TAKE YOUR WORLD

"Thank you, Mr. Luca! A diva like myself tries to take pride in *some* things!"

He removes a pen from his suit pocket and starts signing. "Remember, I'm a silent partner. You have full discretion to do whatever you need to make this business successful. After one year, the contract will end and you should be financially stable."

"I'm so thankful that you came all the way here to help me get my boutique off the ground," I say gratefully.

"You're an excellent businesswoman, so I know you'll do well. Let's go back out to the music. May I have the absolutely *last* dance."

We leave my office and go back to join the rest of the guests. Stepping out onto the dance floor, I have the time of my life! Oh, my goodness, he's a skilled dancer. He glides across the floor with such ease, and is so smooth with his moves. The music stops way too soon and we have to say our goodbyes. Walking him to the door, I tell him to have a safe flight. We promise to keep in touch, as we have a conference call the next week. Thankful to all my guests for coming, I'm glad to know I have *true* supporters. It was truly a momentous event, well except for Tasha's madness! My feet are sore and every part of my body is screaming for a nice hot bubble bath. My mom and sisters are staring at me. I guess they are in such awe of my success.

Mom has to be the one to get misty-eyed. "I'm very proud of you Chanel and all your success. I wish your older sisters would follow in your footsteps. You have made me a proud mama! So proud!" She reaches out to give me a great big hug! I squeeze her as tight as I can. You only got one mother!

"Mama, I love you! I love you too, my dear sisters!"

They both begin to roll their eyes.

"Well, if you love us so much, where're we staying for the night? I mean you got a big house and all!" My oldest sister speaks up.

"I know better, the power of prayer will send you to a hotel."

"The power of prayer? What about the comfort of a king-sized bed

and the entertainment of real cable? I'm not about that hotel life!"

'Well, you better work that thin hotel soap to a nice lather. Have a nice bath!"

"Can we stay with you, please?!" My other sister pleads.

"Y'all snore too damn loud…and you know me and mama *need* our beauty sleep!"

They couldn't help but laugh and concur with me. "True, Sis! We sleep *real* good!"

My assistant Kevin helps me put the boutique back together. All we need is some good team work and the place will look beautiful again. My event planner saunters over to me and remarks, "Well, the night was a success. I even met a potential bae."

Hey! Everybody at this party was pretty turnt up. When she saw the broom in my hand and a dust pan in the other, she snatched them from me.

"I'll help him finish. You go home and relax."

I so appreciate them both. Extremely tired, the only thing on my mind is going home to get some rest.

Oh, no! I forgot about Tasha aka Tess. She's truly a good person, but without medication, she is a mess. That's when I dial Tasha. She picks right up.

"Who is this calling me this late? It's eleven thirty at night. It better not be a booty call!" She raves.

"It's me Chanel. I was just checking up on you to make sure you are okay."

She begins to cry. "You don't care about me! If you did, you would've never asked me to leave. It wasn't even all my fault." Her sobs start to grow louder. She never let me get another word in edgewise. As loud as she can, she screams.

"Get off my phone ex-friend!"

Then I hear several clicks in my ear. At this point, I realize it was Tess. I was not talking to, not Tasha. I'll just let her cool off for a couple of days and get her meds back in her system. Maybe she will come around to her senses.

When I get home, I take a shower and go to bed. A couple days later, I'm in the bed when my phone rings, I realize it is one in the morning. It is my mother calling to say that she had a great time. I can hear my two sisters in the background say, "Love you, sis! We're on our way home from the airport."

"Okay, have a safe trip home and I'll talk to you next week."

Deciding to sleep in, I can't because Mr. Luca calls right after them.

"Thank you for being an outstanding business woman," he says.

That was a short conversation, but I am irritated. If someone else calls me, I'm going to throw the phone against the wall. At that moment, I power my phone off.

Tasha

Let me finish telling the story about *my* Sunday. It will be in my best interest to keep Tess at bay. I'm not a fan of popping pills, because they make me sleepy. Tess enjoys doing her and I enjoy doing me as well. We both can't come out at the same time. Somebody is going to lose. Deciding to skip going to church, because I'm really not feeling it, I stay home. Listening to some smooth jazz, I vibe to Boney James. He's one of my favorites. His music sends me on a wonderful journey of mental freedom. It'll be a great day to cook all my dinners for the week. Should I make chicken piccata with a parmesan risotto, or veggie lasagna with a garden salad? Choices, choices. It's a little early, around 3:07 pm on a hot summer day.

I just lost a game of *Candy Crush* and am ready to beg for some lives. Y'all know how that is! The familiar ringtone of

Jodeci's, '*Come and Talk to Me*' starts blaring through my cell. It's Chase! Yes!

"Good afternoon, beautiful! How was the masquerade party?" Really not wanting to talk about it, I vaguely say, "It was alright. What are you doing today?"

"Trying to finish putting up these posters. I have a lot of headway to make today."

"Why are you doing that?" My curiosity is peaked.

"You know I'm running for mayor. It's a big goal, but I've got *big* dreams. I aim high."

"Awesome. Do you need some help? These hands could come and help volunteer."

"Great. Let me give you my campaign office's address. Can you be there by four?"

"Sure. Let me freshen up a little." Immediately getting off the phone, I run upstairs to take a hot shower. Searching in my panty drawer for my crotch less navy blue, lace panties and matching pushup bra, I'm ready for whatever. I'm dressed in a black pencil skirt and a pink silk ruffled blouse with a plunging neck-line. He isn't going to know how to act when he sees me. After styling my hair, I beat my face for the gods and rush out the door.

Showing up at his campaign office, I see that there is a sign on the door that reads, 'If you need to get in, please use the buzzer'. That's exactly what I do.

"Who is it?" A male's voice asks.

"It's me Chase, Tess." That's when I have to hurry and clean it up. How did that come out my month? Correcting myself, I blurt out, "It's Tasha!" He's only seen Tess. Suddenly, she comes out in full force once he buzzes me in. Chase greets me at the door.

"You're looking mighty fine today! That skirt fits you wonderfully." He beckons for me to come inside.

"You smell good and you're looking good. Damn, baby."

"Thank you, baby girl!" That's when it gets very quiet.

Asking him where everyone is, Chase shares with me that it is just us two. He says everyone left for the day to spend time with their families. As he is giving me a tour of the campaign headquarters, I notice it is actually really nice. The last place we stop is his office. Walking into his office, I notice a beautiful sofa beside his desk. Then my eyes wander and I notice that he has pictures on his desk of a woman and two little boys.

"Who is that?" I question kind of knowing the answer already.

"That's my wife and two sons," he admits right away.

"You look like a very happy family. I'm not into breaking up happy homes."

"Well, I'm *not* happy." Suddenly, Chase walks over to the door and locks it.

"Don't be afraid, Tasha. I won't hurt you."

"I'm not." My eyes move up to capture his, letting him know that I'm ready to ravish him.

He is sitting on the edge of the desk rubbing his hands together greedily as he stares at me.

"My family is out of town. So, it's just me and you."

Casually, I walk closer to him and then start massaging and kissing his neck. He is startled at first, but ends up leaning back into it. There are three neat stacks of posters sitting at the edge of the desk. For dramatics, I slide them onto the floor. Noticing he is starting to get nervous, Tess kicks in.

"I want that sexy body, right here, right now." After letting that be known, I start unbuckling his belt, then pull down his zipper. His pants slide down to the ground, touching the floor. That's when he leans back on the desk and enjoys every minute of the master blow job I deliver.

"Damn Tasha," he groans with his fingers in my hair. "Uhh..."

Working up enough spit, I take him deep down my throat and start to gargle. That is all he can take as he is climaxing in no time. Before I know it, I can feel his member start to pulsate and then his seeds spew down my throat. Instead of being repulsed, I swallow every single ounce like he's my man. Soon, he will be.

Tess has skills honey.

When he is done, he pulls me up, turns me around and starts pulling my dress over my head. He slowly pulls down my panties and my body is on fire. The only thing I have on is my six-inch stilettos. He lifts my feet out of them, one at a time. I am standing there with only my bra on. Then Chase grabs me by the back of my head and tongues me down. The taste of his sweet tongue has me craving more and more of him. Our kisses start to grow more intense. He bends me over the desk and spreads my legs open. He then proceeds to drop to his knees. Feeling his blazing tongue on my feverish skin, I close my eyes.

"Mmm… yes… Chase…" My moans are loud as he moves up to the treasure he craves.

My hands are clutching the edge of desk for dear life, because this man is gobbling me up like a snack.

"You taste so good…" His voice trails off as he sucks and licks.

In no time, I am nearing an explosive orgasm.

"I'm almost there… Ohhh… That's it, baby…" The tingles spread to the tips of my toes.

My entire body is weak and feel like mush by the time he turns me around. When he kisses me again, I can taste my essence on his tongue. He pulls away from me and I lick my lips.

"Oh, I can't wait to be inside you," Moaning against my lips, he lifts me up and sits me down on top of the desk. Then he enters me slowly.

"Wow…" My breath catches in my throat. "Chase… ohhh…"

He is so well-endowed that it feels as if he was stretching my walls to capacity.

"Are you okay baby?" Peeking down at me, the pleasure on his face lets me know that he is hoping I am.

"Yes… don't stop… Ohhh… my…god!" My eyes roll back because he was touching spots I never even knew were there. Damn, my legs were shaking and all.

Chase's tongue is on my collarbone and then my nipples are in his mouth, being devoured one by one.

Tossing my head back, I'm on cloud nine on my way to heaven's door.

"Tasha… oh…myyyy… You are the best… I can't hold on any longer baby…" His voice is deep and raspy.

Part of me wants to tell him that it's Tess rocking his world, not Tasha, but I keep quiet. Instead, I decide to ride the orgasm wave with him.

"Let's cum together…" I coax in his ear before softly nibbling his earlobe.

Oh my, I'd desperately needed his touch. Our bodies move in perfect harmony. When we are done, my body feels so light. I sure came good.

"It's been a long time since I've been with a man. Just to feel your touch. Oooh! You were amazing." Our lips touch and ignite a flame again.

"I really enjoyed you! You touched spots on my body that my wife never even tried to touch!" His hands are softly caressing my ass cheeks.

Chase reaches behind his desk where there is a small refrigerator and asks me what I would like to drink. He starts to name off various kinds of alcohol.

"I have some white wine, red wine, vodka, cognac and tequila." Because the freak had already come out of me. I'm Tess and not Tasha," I say, "Let me get something hard like some tequila!"

He pours me a drink and then asks, "Are you hungry?" He passes me a stack of restaurant menus. "Order whatever you want."

We had worked up an appetite.

Among the menus that he gave me is one of my favorite Chinese spots. We both order the Egg Fu Yung and fried rice. Our food finally arrives and we scarf it down so fast that I bit down on my tongue. We just relax and sit back listening to music with our bellies full.

He notices it is getting late, but the both of us are still sitting there getting to know one another. It is after one am by the time we wrap up our night. Chase explains that he has a big meeting at ten am. He walks me to my car, passionately kisses me, opens my car door and says goodnight. Then I speed off on the way home. The whole time driving home, I really wonder what Chase wants with me. He's handsome, successful, intelligent and married. "

Chase

What did I just do? Why am I trying to mess up my happy home…everything I built?

My wife will kill me if she ever finds out I had sex with another woman. Making up my mind that I will never see Tasha again, once I get home, I immediately jump in the shower, take off all my clothes and wash her away forever. After I'm all done, I get in the bed and about an hour after that my phone rings. Looking up at the red numbers on my alarm clock, I notice it is after three am.

"Chase, I love you so much. You just don't know!"

"Who is this?"

"It's me baby, Tasha! We just made love. How can you not recognize my voice?"

"We just had sex. You don't love me and I don't love you. You better get off my damn phone! Good night!"

"I do! I do!"

After that, I realize that chick is crazy. What the hell have I done?

Tasha

The next morning all I can think about is Chase. It is about four in the evening and I'm on my way home from work. Chase has not called me all day. I am starting to become fire red mad. He thinks he's going to play me after what we did last night? My plan is blow up his cell until he talks to me. What? He keeps sending *me* straight to voicemail. Fifteen calls later and still no answer? Chase is starting to bring out the worse in me... um Tess! Tess does all the talking now... She is in full control.

"If your boo doesn't answer the phone, drive up to his job. He can hardly resist how sexy you are!" There the voice is again in my head, making me go against my will.

Trying my best to persuade Tess, I say, "Maybe we shouldn't do this."

"Oh yes! We are going to do this!' We 'bout to show Chase who run this!

My next stop is Chase's campaign office.

A flashback of last night returned to my mind. The sex was so good. Chase touched spots on my body that I forgot were still working. He told me that my body is hot, wet and juicy. He enjoyed *me* caressing, rubbing and licking all over his body. Reaching the campaign office, I see all types of media outlets there. Walking inside, I notice Chase is accompanied by the former mayor. I hear him say "Congratulations, you're the next mayor of our city!"

He gives Chase the key to the city.

Catching a glimpse of me, suddenly Chase stops smiling. He casually walks through the crowd toward me. He passes his campaign manager and tells him to give him a minute. When he reaches me, he motions for me to follow him. As soon as we reach his office, he closes the door angrily behind him. I can tell he is pissed off, but I couldn't care less.

"What are you doing here? So, you're a stalker now? And on a day like today!"

"I missed you and I just wanted to see your face."

"I can never see you again. Last night was a mistake. I'm the mayor now. I'm married. I can't mess this up." Once he tells me that, I feel completely devastated.

"How can you do this to me? I thought you cared for me."

"Why would you think that? I never told you that. You were just a one-night-stand. My wife is on her way. You gotta get the hell out of here." Trying to keep his voice low, he looks around like he was all paranoid.

"You told me you aren't happy with her. The things your wife won't do, I will!" Reaching up to grab his crotch, he grips my wrist before I can.

With an evil glint in his eyes, he says, "I don't want you…just leave… and now?"

"So, why wasn't you thinking about your wife when you were hitting it from the back? Why wasn't you thinking about your wife when I was giving you head and you came in my mouth? Where was she then? Where?! Where?! Where?!"

His lack of response is making my blood pressure boil. I'm so upset that I want to hurt somebody.

"If you don't leave willingly, I will have security escort you out."

Breaking down in sobs, my stomach is in knots. It hurts so bad. How could he do this to me? How? How? And why is my phone ringing now? I don't want to talk, but I need to answer it.

"Hello."

"Hey girl…"

A familiar voice. It is Chanel

"Hey girl! How're you doing?"

"I'm about to catch a case!"

"Who is this? It must be Tess…Tasha don't talk like that."

"Does it matter who it is. Okay, It's Tess, Chanel! Why are you calling if you know who it is?"

"Wait a minute. I know I can get through to my best friend. Tasha…if you can hear me, please tell me where you are."

"At the mayor's campaign. Look at the news. It's a live broadcast.

Please, don't hang up." The call disconnects.

After crying in Chase's office for about ten minutes, I wipe my face and walk out into the main area. He is standing behind the podium bragging about what he will do for the community as mayor. Standing next to him proudly is his wife. That really pisses me off. How could he be standing here with her? He was rocking my body last night. What a phony. Who chose him as the mayor? If his wife, or precious *community* ever found out about me, he'd be forced to step down. Nah! That's too easy. I go outside to my car, pop the trunk, reach underneath my spare tire and grab my gun. After cocking it, I stroll back inside with all the confidence I can muster. Men like him need to be taught a lesson.

He is never ever going to hurt another woman like he did me again. No one is paying attention to me, as I casually move up to the front. Chase is looking so full of himself behind that podium. Someone needs to wipe that smirk off his face. Raising the gun, I point it straight at Chase.

Pop! Pop! Pop!

When the shots ring out, the sound startles me, and I jolt back. People scatter like roaches.

Dropping the gun to the floor, I wipe the sweat from my face. Just like that, Chase's lifeless body crumbles to the floor. Immediately, I am surrounded by about four police officers. One forces me down to the ground, places her knee on my back and yells, "Don't move!"

Everyone is running for their lives and taking cover. Chase's wife is shouting, "My husband's been shot! Call 911! Call 911!"

Pulling my free hand away from my back, I point at her.

"Your husband deserved everything he got! He needs to burn in hell I can't believe I let that dickhead play me!" Then, I faintly hear the voice of a woman. The woman is telling the officer that she has information about me that will help the investigation.

It's Chanel. She's screaming. "Oh my! That's my best friend, Tasha! Tasha, why did you do that?"

She came to see about me as promised. That's my ace. As they are handcuffing me and reading me my rights, Chanel tries to make eye contact with the officer.

"Officer, she takes medication. She's not in her right mind "

The officer nods, "Please explain."

"That's my best friend. She hides her split personalities. It's sort of like a mask of deception. When she takes her medication, she acts nothing like this. This is totally uncharacteristic of her. I love her very much. Please help her."

The officer then suggests that Chanel follow them. In light of the information that she provided, I'm going to have a psychological evaluation.

Chanel

With Tasha now locked up, what am I going to do? How could Tess do this to Tasha…I cannot understand why. As I walk into the psych wing of the hospital, I feel the hair stand on the back of my neck. The place freaks me out. The entrance door has no window and an intercom. There is also a timer and multiple video cameras placed at each angle. You would think I am visiting a maximum-security prison. The front desk attendant checks my purse and any personal items that I have on me. Is this place serious, or what? Once I am deemed *clear,* the nurse leads me to the room Tasha is placed in. Tasha is wearing yellow scrubs, which is standard garb for new patients. She is lying back on the bed, propped against a pillow watching television. There are two doctors standing on each side of her bed. I approach the doctor that looks friendly.

"Can I check up on her later? I know that I'm not next of kin, but I'm all she has," I explain wholeheartedly feeling for my friend.

"Do you know how we can reach her family? It's against HIPAA laws for me to share her condition with you. I'd be sued as well as the hospital."

"Yes, sir. I understand. Her parents are deceased. I'll reach out to her cousin."

Later I call Tasha's cousin and she's devastated by the news. They send their prayers and give me formal consent to get information about Tasha's medical condition. This is too stressful! Never have I been in such an awkward position. My best friend is in a psych ward after shooting the mayor.

Two days later, I call Tasha's doctor to get an update. The doctor tells me that her prognosis is not good.

"Tasha is going to be committed permanently for the violent crime she committed. At this point she is delusional and unresponsive."

"So, you're saying she won't recognize me?"

"That's correct," he confirms.

That's when I break down crying.

"Feel free to call and check up on her. If you want to visit her, give it about two weeks."

Those were the longest two weeks of my life. Keeping her in my prayers, I hoped for a miracle. Now is finally the time to go see her. I will try my hardest to be positive. My nerves are completely wrecked. Three years ago, she told me that if she ever ended up back in the psych ward for more than two days, to request a release from her lease at her apartment. Tasha wanted to donate all her stuff to the Salvation Army. Calling my mom, my sister and all our close friends, I break the news to them that Tasha has been committed to a psych hospital indefinitely. They express their deepest concerns and promise to forever keep her in their prayers.

Arriving at the hospital in the afternoon, I am taken into a private room where Tasha is sitting in a wheelchair, looking up at the ceiling. Her hair is a hot mess and her nails look like she has been in a war. She keeps repeating, "He thought I was playing," over and over. Sitting down in a chair right in front of her, I clear my throat and try to say something to her without breaking down and crying.

"Hey, Tasha! Are you okay?"

She hears my voice, slowly looks into my eyes, and then her face is blank. She just stares without saying one word. Then she picks back up where she left off. "He thought I was playing." At that moment, I realize Tasha is no more. Immediately, I get up and run out crying. I slow down before I get to the door, almost missing her doctor. He taps my shoulder before I sign out my personal items.

"That was a very short visit, Chanel."

"There is no way I can take seeing Tasha like that. It breaks my heart," I admit

He nods in understanding, "The physicians and other hospital staff will take very good care of her. Call anytime."

"Thank you again for your kindness! I have to go now…goodbye." Without looking back, I head to my car.

Unfortunately, the mayor died from his gunshot wounds. He'd just lost too much blood and they couldn't save him. It hurt me to know that my friend had succumbed to her mental illness and Tess.

However, regardless of how I feel about my best friend Tasha, I have to focus on my business. There was a very nice article written about my boutique in the business section of the Memphis Tribune the week before and business was booming.

Days go by and then months. Before I know it, a year had passed. Deciding to use my blessings for a good cause, I founded a domestic violence charity and named it, Tasha aka Tess – A Life That Was Lost Foundation. I never went back to that hospital ever again, because I just couldn't take seeing Tasha that way. She'd once been so full of life and promise. Not long after that, I paid Mr. Luca Sullo off. Life went on, but I never once stopped thinking about and missing my best friend.

IT'S A KITTY AND DOGGIE WORLD

This chapter is for all you men out there. Have you ever thought to yourself, can a cat impregnate a dog? No, that's not biologically possible. Well, ladies, harness the kitty, never expecting to get dogged. My name is Ms. Dunja Moss. Yeah, my first name is very unusual. If you Google my name, you will see that it means, a fruit.

My mother would always say, "One day, Dunja you'll blossom into a beautiful woman."

That day is now, since I'm twenty-two years old. Finally, I am finished pursuing my degree in business management. Deciding to follow in my mother's footsteps, I am pursuing a career in real estate.

I'd finally received my results for my final exams. They were all in the ninety percentile, so that boosted up my GPA. My mom and I celebrate at the five-star restaurant of my choice. Mother has the octopus and I have lobster. The food is delicious, and we really have a great time. My mom and I are really close. By the way my, my mother's name is Ms. Danielle Moss. Let me give you the tea about my mother and my life. That way you'll have a clear understanding about how I was born. My mother raised me by herself. Never knowing my father, I kept begging my mother to tell me who he is. It just fell on deaf ears, so I eventually just stopped asking.

My mother provided me with the best life and education. I spoke three different languages including, English, Spanish and French. We would always travel together during the summer. Our destinations included Rome, Venice, Paris, Costa Rica, and London. In the winter we would go skiing in Aspen, Vail, or Mt. Baker. My life has been complete in every way. The only thing that is missing is romance. One thing I'd always wanted is to meet a real man who'd sweep me off my feet. The thing is, I have to put myself out there to meet that man. So, I make a promise to myself that I'll start dating this year.

Just wanting a man to spoil and pamper me, is my desire. Making sweet love to me all night would only be a bonus. That isn't asking for too much, is it? A girl can always fantasize, right? It'll happen for me one day, since every thot I know has a man. Not able to get it out of mind, or my heart, my desire to know who my father only seemed to grow.

Daydreaming, I wonder if we look alike, or have anything in common? Something tells me I will never know. My mother is one of the top real estate agents in Houston, TX. She's had her own business for twenty years. Most of her competition, agents and clients would consider my mother a beast of a businesswoman. She knew what to do to close on a house quickly and efficiently. Also, she could charm the pants off a man, and most of the time she did. So, basically you can say mother has two types of skills. I'd learned from the best. Most of the time, I watched my mother work her charm while selling houses. Whether the property cost fifteen thousand dollars, or two million, she got the job done. All her clients love her. My mother would give all her clients who closed a Tiffany's gift bag. You never knew what was in it. It was a surprise.

Now you see why they call her a great business woman. My mother made good decisions, and bad decisions. Mostly everyone can relate to that, right? Those bad decisions did not bother me much, or make me not want to be just like my mother. She took me under her wing, and taught me everything I know about the real estate business. The thing is, she did not expect for me to catch on so quick.

Next thing I know, mother announces to me and her staff that she is retiring. Now I have to frantically start looking for an executive assistant. I need my mother's assistant to teach my new executive quick. It takes me two weeks to find my executive assistant. Her name is Rose Trevino. She's Italian and came highly recommended by my girlfriend Lee Lee. The two of us hit it off very well in no time.

What I like about Rose is she's really organized. She walks around with a notebook in her hand at all times and she's very efficient. Hopefully she's ready for the job. Sometimes my business life interferes with my social life. At times, I can't keep my men in order. The thought makes me chuckle to myself and I have a huge smile on my face. It's 2017 and about time women flip the script on men.

A few weeks later I threw my mother a big retirement party. Everyone she knows and loves was invited. Not only did she have the time of her life, but she was lit as if she was twenty years old. My mother decided she wanted to buy a summer home in Italy from Rose's uncle. It was the first day of summer when my mother and I flew to Italy to close the deal on my mother's new home. Mother gave me the opportunity to be her agent, because she wanted to see if I could handle the profession.

Everything went great and I received a hefty commission. Rose's uncle Butch Trevino and my mother were very happy with me. Deciding to stay for a week to help mother set up her new home, I had the time of my life. By the time I left, mother's house was finished from bottom to top.

The day has come for me to leave. Mother drops me off at the airport. Sharing long hugs, we both start to cry. Mother lets me know she will see me in two months. I walk in the airport not believing it when it takes over thirty minutes to get through security. Getting to my gate on time, I thank God, I am sitting by myself. Listening to the old school jam, "Makin' Good Love" by Avant, I text Rose. As I press the keys, I let her know that I will be landing by 9 p.m. and to notify my driver that I'm not coming into the Houston, TX- hobby airport but going to IAH. When I hired Rose, I told her that I have a pet peeve about my car not being on time. God forbids if it is an emergency, she better be sure she calls me, or she will be out the door. Everyone has had one or two pink slips, or should I say has had walking papers.

She must always make sure my driver picks me up from the airport on time. Suddenly, my small suitcase fell on my new Red Bottoms. Quickly, I pull out my ear buds, ready to punch this dude in his throat after reading his ass. Deciding to cuss him out in Spanish, I say, "Cabeza de verga," which means dickhead. Before I can get another word out, this fine, gorgeous man with a nice smile apologizes. Ladies this man stands at least six feet tall and has on a white linen, silk suit that is tailored made. On his feet are fresh black Gators.

This man is looking good and smelling even better. Very sophisticated indeed, that is what attracts me to him the most, along with his swag. Totally forgetting about being mad at him, I drift thinking I'd love to get my freak on with him. He immediately extends his hand. Extending mine for a handshake, I am spellbound when he kisses it instead.

"Hi, my name is Mr. SeBay Day." Introducing himself, he stares deeply into my eyes.

In my mind his nickname is, "Sugar Daddy" because he looks a little older than me.

Flirting with me, he says, "I don't see a ring on your finger."

I say to myself, 'I see a huge ring on your left ring finger.' He quickly asks me, "Should I call you mademoiselle, or Madame?"

My response is, "Just call me Madame." Madame gives off the impression that I'm a grown woman and not a little girl. My desire to rip his clothes off and show him what a grown woman like me can do is extremely strong. Of course, I have to pull back. He is just sitting there with a sly, sexy grin on his face.

He then asks me in a baritone voice, "What is your name, sexy?"

By now I'm tongue-tied because he is so hot. Managing to find my voice, I tell him, "My name is Ms. Dunja Moss."

"That a beautiful name. What's the meaning behind it?"

Sharing with him the story my mother gave me behind the name, I notice that he is licking his lips. It is almost like he is undressing me with his eyes. My body is starting to flush with unadulterated passion. It's been a long time and I could feel the pulsating tremble between my thighs. Getting even hotter, my heart is thumping so hard against my ribcage. Needing to pause, I take a deep breath. All I want to do is jump on him and ride him like a jockey. Once I'm done with him, he'll be begging for more.

"You'll never get rid of him; just like a roach," I say to myself. What I could do to that man and the huge piece of meat I know he is packing.

After you dog them out, send them back home. I'd learned that tip from my mother. She would always say, "It's hard out here for a pimp." It was hard for me to understand what that meant, until I got older. When I started dealing with men, it all made sense.

We continue talking and the gate agent calls zone one. We notice that we both are flying first class.

He says, "You are going to love these flatbeds." It is obvious we are attracted to one another, since we keep checking each other out on our way on the plane. He immediately finds his seat and sits his baggage down. After that, he quickly goes to the restroom. That's when I kick into action and ask the guy who is sitting next to him if we can switch seats. Coming up with an outrageous story, I say, "The gate agent made a mistake and put my husband and I in separate seats. We just got married today."

Wow, I'm so good, I should have been an actress.

The guy is very gracious. "I would not want to separate love. Sure, you can have my seat," he obliges.

Thanking him with a big smile, I notice Sebay returning from the restroom with a puzzled expression on his face.

He says, "Well, what a coincidence that we are sitting next to each other."

At this point I'm licking my lips. The captain announces that we are next in line to take off. It takes fourteen hours and thirty minutes to get home. What a long flight, but I had so much fun talking to Sebay. When I asked him what he did for a living, he explained that he owns a fleet of boats in Houston, Texas.

That was a good time for me to let him know that I loved water skiing. "Maybe we can meet at your dock sometime and go waterskiing. What do you think?" That's when I reach into my purse to grab a business card for him. In return, he passes me his business card.

"I'm looking for a commercial property in Houston. Can I give you a call next Thursday at around three pm, so we can discuss some property?" He asks with a sexy smile.

My response is, "Sure, I'll put you on my calendar. My executive assistant Rose will contact you to set up an appointment to look at a few properties."

"Fantastic," he mutters with a smile on his face. "I look forward to seeing you next week."

After giving him a big hug, we head off the plane. It is a surprise that he hugs me back. My body pressed into his body felt so good. That hug has me fantasizing about what I can do to him. Imagining licking him all over, his voice interrupts my fantasy. "Well, it was my pleasure Dunja. We'll talk soon."

We say our goodbyes and go our separate ways. I'm still envisioning what I'd do to him behind closed doors. All I want to do is rip his clothes off and see that hard body in the flesh. As I'm walking to baggage claim, my cell phone rings.

It is mother.

"Dunja, did you make it home safely?"

"Yes mother," I reply in a sarcastic tone.

That woman acts like I'm a baby, or something.

"Okay, I'm just checking up on you. I'm going back to sleep. Love you."

"Ti amo!" I tell her in Italian and then end the call.

Since mother let me take over her business in downtown Houston, Texas and gave me her house, I have big girl panties to fill. It is time to make, power moves just like my mother had. As soon as I grab my luggage, my phone rings again. This time it is Rose.

"Your limo is outside in front waiting for you."

"Thank you. I'll see you on Monday."

"Have a good weekend Ms. Dunja."

On Monday, when I arrive in the office, Rose has a hot cup of cappuccino waiting for me and my itinerary for the day sitting on my desk. That is what I call a great executive assistant. She's handling her business, which makes her job secure. Immediately using the intercom, I ask Rose to step into my office. Her reply is, "I'm on my way Ms.Dunja."

Once she's standing in front of me, I explain, "Call my new client, Mr. Sebay."

"He left a voice message over the weekend asking if he can move the appointment to a Wednesday at three pm," she informs me.

"Call him and let him know that I'll be sending him an email today. I need him to fill out a profile sheet letting me know what areas he's interested in and price range."

Rose smiles at me. "I'm amazed at how you still pull clients, even on your vacation. One day I want to be just like you."

Chuckling, I say, "I'm not sure if you're ready for all this kind of work."

"I'll take care of it right away." She smiles.

"Thank you," I tell her before she scurries off to her desk.

Rose isn't at her desk for more than five minutes before she buzzes my intercom.

"You have a call on line one, Miss Dunja. He said his name is Reece."

"Please take a message Rose."

She comes back and says, "He said he's not getting off the phone until you talk to him."

I'm starting to lose my patience with this guy and don't know why he sweats me so bad. Picking up the phone, I have a real attitude.

"Reece what do you want? I'm working."

"Baby, I been looking for you down at the club. The last time I saw you was when I came to you crib two weeks ago to cook dinner for you."

"Dinner was great too. Those barbecue ribs, potato salad, baked beans, and cornbread were finger licking good. So, what up boo?"

My pet name for him is "Hood Man."

"Just tryna please you baby."

After we ate dinner that night, I told him that I had to wash a load of clothes. Too tired to do it, he did it for me while I relaxed on the sofa.

"What happened? Did you lose my number?" He sounds so pitiful, I almost feel sorry for him.

"Baby let me call you back. I just got into the office, so we'll have to talk later."

"Okay, baby girl. You so fine. I just miss those thick legs and that hot, deep, wet..."

"Boy get off my phone!" This negro is whipped.

Just the sound of his voice does something to me though, I must admit. Not only is his voice a turn on, but he's also a fine, tall hunk of sexy chocolate. Standing 6'5, he's one of those buff men whose penis didn't shrink in the process of working out. That man was working with a monster.

"Mmm, I just want to feel you again. I want to be so deep inside you your knees get so weak that when we done, you can't walk."

"Okay, that's enough Reese." With a flirtatious giggle, I tell him that I have to go.

Fifteen minutes goes by and my assistant buzzes me again, "Ms. Dunja, you have a call on line two. It's Mr. Jobert."

"Hello."

"Hey baby, how're you doing?"

"I'm good."

"I miss you. What color underwear are you wearing?"

"I'm not wearing any," I decide to entice him for my entertainment.

"Mmm... you know I got something big and hard waiting for you."

The thought sends tingles up and down my spine, but I have to get off the phone and get something done.

"I'm at work now, David. I have to get some work done today."

"I understand that, but I want to work you…"

Is it a full moon or something? The freaks are coming out early this morning.

"So, how was your weekend?" I ask, trying to get him off the sex talk. My panties were already soaked and I had a whole work day ahead.

"Could have been better if you were with me Dunja."

My nickname for him is, "College Man."

"How your mother's doing? Does she like her new house?" He asks.

"Yes, it's beautiful."

He changes the subject. "I can't wait to see you. Are you coming over tonight?" "Yes baby, I miss seeing you," I confirm.

"Okay, how about you come to my place at six? Is that cool?"

"Yes."

"I got a treat for you tonight, baby. I'm in a freaky mood, so bring the handcuffs and some whipped cream."

Knowing what that means, I'm in for a treat.

"I got that all covered baby. See you soon."

Then I buzz Rose. "Hold all my calls unless it's my mother."

"Yes ma'am."

Before I know it, it is already 5 o' clock. Lord, let me get my butt up out of this office so I can prepare for my night. As I'm walking out of my office, I say my good night to Rose. Rushing home, I quickly take a shower, get dressed and grab my bag of goodies.

Before driving all the way to David's house, I decide to call and make sure he is home. He picks up on the first ring.

"Baby, are you on your way?"

"Umm, David, you're being a little thirsty."

"Just bring your fine butt on. Dinner's ready and you're my dessert."

We both start to laugh. His is lustful and mine is flirtatious. After ending the call, it doesn't take very long to get to David's house. He greets me at the door with a glass of wine. Soft music is playing and candles are lit throughout the house.

"I hope you're hungry and prepared for a feast. You know I just finished culinary arts school."

With a nod, I feed his ego, "Yes baby and you are one of the best chefs in Houston Texas."

"That's right," he agrees before kissing my wine flavored lips. "Dunja, why don't you go on upstairs and get comfortable. You know, slip into something sexy."

If he wants sexy, that's exactly what he'll get. The black cat suit is tight as a glove with thin spaghetti straps. The way it fits me, he is going to see every detail of my body down to my camel toe.

By the time I get downstairs, he has changed out of his clothes. The only thing that he has on is his chef's hat, an apron and his boxers. That is easy access, so let's get it on. It is like I am at a five-star restaurant. David pulls my chair out like a true gentleman.

He does everything I ask, and who wouldn't love that? David has prepared baked Dijon salmon with stuffed crab, lobster tails with Teen's Spicy Pesto Chicken, and Pasto with Italian potatoes and spinach. For desert, he prepared my favorite, Veiled Maiden (apple cream parfait).

"Mmm, that was fantastic," I tell him when I'm all done. My plate is clean because I'm not one of those chicks who are afraid to eat in front of a man.

After sampling all the food, I am so full, I'm ready for a nap. That's when David says, "I'm ready for dessert baby."

Standing up from the table, he undresses me, picks me up and sits me down on the kitchen counter. Grabbing the can of whipped cream, he stares at me slyly before spraying some on my inner thigh.

"Mmm…" he moans before slipping down to his knees.

As he slurps and licks every trace of whipped cream from my feverish skin, I can't help but grab the back of his head.

"Ohhh…" In anticipation of feeling his tongue between my thighs, I lead him down further.

When his tongue touches that spot, he gently sucks and licks me into oblivion. I'm humping his face and working hard for my release. Moving my pelvis in circles, I close my eyes feeling the tingles of an amazing orgasm.

"Yesss… David… yessss…"

"I wanna taste every single drop…" His voice is so sexy and I'm ready for something large and stiff. From there we end up in the living room on the floor in front of the fireplace. He enters me gently and we tear it up all over that floor. He pulls my hair and spanks me as he hits it from the back.

"Dunja, ohhh…mmm…"

"Uhhh… David… yessss baby!"

You can see where we left a few wet spots on the living room carpet.

"Mmm… you feel so good," he moans as he kisses me deeply.

Then he picks me up again and we end up in the bedroom.

"Bring out the handcuffs baby. I want you to take control. Cuff me."

While I'm cuffing his wrists to the bed posts, he says, "Let's play a game. We can call it cops and robbers. You're the cop and caught me. Now you can rob my body."

"You don't have to tell me twice," I purr, climbing on top of his fine ass.

Once I've straddled him, I position my body so that I can take him deep inside of me.

"Ohhh…" Immediately, I'm feeling all types of pleasure riveting over my anatomy.

"Wow… you're the best I ever had… arrrghhh Dunja." David stares up at me in awe as I work my body on top of him like a snake.

His large, warm hands are all over my flesh and so is his tongue.

The wet, juicy sounds fill the room along with our moans. In no time we explode together. When we are finished, we are both exhausted.

"Let's take a nice hot bath," I suggest.

"Go head baby. Get that water prepared. Can you take the cuffs off me now?" That's when I jump out of bed and say slyly, "I'll be back.".."

"Baby, bring your big butt back here and take these cuffs off me, girl. I need to take a leak!" It's not hard to tell that he's getting big mad.

He starts to yell my name, "Dunja, Dunja! Come on! It's not funny!"

Quickly, I go back to the bed and take off the handcuffs.

"You play too much, baby."

Not able to hold my laughter in, I walk away sexily switching my hips. We end up in the Jacuzzi. We get out of the water and dry off. Before he can drift off to sleep, I return the favor and give him the best head of his life.

"Damn… Dunja!"

Pushing himself deep down my throat, he thrusts his pelvis anxiously for his nut.

Taking his babies into my mouth, I get up and make my way to the bathroom. Then I spit in the sink and rinse my mouth out with mouthwash. Once I make it back to bed, I notice that he is already snoring. Shaking my head, I join him and in no time, I'm in la la land myself.

When I wake up the next morning, David is up already. He serves me a light breakfast in bed. This man really knows how to spoil me, and I don't have to do too much for him. All I have to do is look good, smell good and make good loving to him. That's when I have a flashback about Reece from the hood. I'll be seeing him on Saturday at the club. You know I'm going to carry my gun since I have to drive through the 5th Ward. There are some good people down there, but a lady just has to watch her back. David tries to climb into bed for round two. That's when my cell phone rings.

David asks with a pissed off look on his face, "Who is calling you so early in the morning? They sure do know how to mess up the moment."

"It's my assistant Rose," I tell him annoyed.

"Good morning Ms. Dunja. Mr. Sebay called and would like to invite you to lunch on Wednesday at noon."

"Check my schedule and see if I have anything set up?"

"Your schedule's open. He also wanted me to tell you to bring your swimsuit. He said you wanted to do some jet skiing. He said after three you can show him the property."

"Call him back and tell him that would be great."

I'm in there like swimwear and can't wait until the next day.

Suddenly, my mind starts drifting off and I am thinking about Sebay.

"I'll miss you baby," Dave's voice invades my fantasies.

"I'll miss you too."

Then I head home to freshen up.

That fine ass Sebay is on my mind the entire time. Calling Rose, I let her know I'll be in the office in about twenty minutes. When I get to the office, Rose walks over to me and says, "You have a full day today. Your first closing is at ten, and your next one is at three."

"Will do," I say cheerfully. "Make sure you order food for each of the closings."

Her response is, "Yes Ms. Dunja, do you want the usual?"

"Yes. Quiche for the ten o'clock and sushi for the three o' clock. Please make sure they send my green tea. The last time they forgot it."

"Yes, I'll take care that." She nods and walks off.

After making a huge commission, I get back to the office and let Rose know she can take the rest of the day off with pay.

She is so happy she runs up to me, gives me a hug and says, "Thank you."

"No problem. Thank you on how you handled the closings for me today. Everything went smoothly."

As I'm driving home, I can't get Sebay out of my mind. When I get there, I realize I have not unpacked from my trip. Pulling my swimsuit out of my luggage, I decide to pack a small bag with a bunch of goodies. I'm smart enough to make sure he wraps it up, so I won't catch anything. Of course, I'm creative, so I bought the condoms that taste like fruit.

Being that I had a long day, I am in bed at seven o' clock pm. Hitting snooze on my alarm, I wake up at eight in the morning. After I am showered and dressed, I realize that I don't have the address for the dock. Immediately, I call my assistant Rose. The whole time I'm saying, please pick up. She picks up on the second ring.

"Good morning, Ms. Dunja, is everything okay?"

"Yes, but I don't have the address for where I'm meeting Mr. Sebay."

"No worries, I'll send a text message with the address."

"Kudos, you're the best executive assistant in the world." When I get behind the wheel, Rose texts me the address and Sebay's private cell phone number. After putting the address in my GPS, I program Sebay's number in my phone's contacts. Then I press the button and say, "Siri…"

"Yes, Dunja," she says in her British accent.

"Call Sebay."

This phone is way too smart.

The phone starts to ring and Sebay answers right away.

"Good afternoon, this is Mr. Sebay."

Just listening to his voice is making me tremble with desire. "Hi, this is Dunja."

"I know, being that I set a ring tone for your number."

"Wow you're making me feel so special."

"You haven't seen anything yet. I've planned a special day for you. Are you ready?"

"Yes," my eyes light up with excitement. "I'll be there shortly."

"Fantastic. I can't wait to see you."

My heart is racing, and my mind is trying to figure out what he has planned for me. Guess, I'll just have to find out later. It is a perfect day at about eighty five degrees. My air is booming in my 2017 fully loaded Mercedes-Benz truck as I groove to some music.

Suddenly, my cell phone rings. It sounds like sirens. That's nobody but Reece, because that's his ringtone. I chose that ringtone for him because he's so hood.

"What's up soft and sexy?" He calls me that because he says my lips are soft and sexy.

"On my way to meet a client."

"I'll stop by your crib when you're done."

He needs to get in line with the rest of these guys. It's not his day of the week, so I let him know. "I'm sorry Reese, but I will be busy for the rest of the night."

That's when he says, 'I'm a little salty with you baby. When I called you last night, your phone went straight to voicemail. Wassup with that?"

Thinking fast on my feet, I say sweetly, "You did baby? My phone was powered off when I woke up in the morning. Uh, Reece, I have to go because I'm pulling up in front of my client's office now. "

He sounds desperate when he asks, "You going to call me later baby?"

"I'm not really sure how long this meeting will run," I admit.

"Dunja, I'll see you on Saturday at the club, right? Your VIP table will be ready at ten, so bring your girls.

"Thanks boo. I'll see you there."

Finally, he is off my line begging.

That man has nothing else to do other than call me? He's getting on my nerves.

Giving him some of this good loving may not have been a good idea because now I can't get rid of him. Making it to the dock, I can see people waterskiing and jet skiing. I grab my light travel baggage from the back of my truck and start to walk toward the dock. This man is standing in front of the dock as I am walking. He's holding a sign with my name on it. Walking up to him, I say, "Hi."

He introduces himself as Captain Fisher. "You must be Dunja?"

"Yes."

"Wow, you look beautiful. Are you ready for an awesome day?"

"Yes, I'm very excited." By now, I can see Sebay waving from a boat and motioning for me to come to him.

Once I step onto the yacht, Sebay immediately gives me a hug. "I almost forgot how beautiful you are. You look sexy."

Most men love me because I'm 5'10 with long legs and a nice, big butt. I'm rocking, short silk shorts and working these four-inch heels. There's a red scarf tied around my neck off to the side and a red, button down blouse that shows a little bit of my cleavage. The look I am going for is classy, but not cheap and not too thirsty. Guess I really pulled it off, since he gave me a great compliment. Lord, this man is too damn fine. He looks good and smells even better. The swagger that he displays is super sexy. Drifting off into my thoughts, I fantasize having some of the best sex of my life with him.

"Thank you and smile, Ms. Dunja."

Looking into his clear brown eyes, I say, "You don't have to be so formal. You can just call me Dunja."

"And you can call me Sebay." He kisses my hand. "Lovely lady, may I have this dance?" Taking me by the hand, he leads me to the back of the yacht. At that point, I still don't hear any music. Then I spot the live band and they start playing "Pretty Wings" by

Maxwell, which is one of my favorite songs. My mother would play that song over and over again. Actually, I know the words by heart. While we are dancing, I start to sing along. "Are you surprised?" Sebay asks as he smiles down at me.

"Yes," I have a huge grin on my face too.

We dance for about five more songs as we start to pull away from the dock.

"I hope you brought your appetite, because I hired a chef to prepare our meal today."

We sit down at the table and the idiot server attempts to put a white napkin in my lap. Immediately, I snatch it off my lap and throw it on the table. "Don't you see that I have on black shorts. I don't want all that white lint all over them."

My close friends always say I go overboard and sometimes they call me Ms. Boogie. I have to calm myself down.

The food is an awesome mixture of seafood and Chinese. We both have one glass of white wine and decide to wait about an hour before we go jet skiing. We finish dinner and Sebay lets me know that he'd like for me to meet the chef that prepared the food.

He says, "We can thank him for the fantastic meal." He tells the server to go downstairs and tell the chef to come up. Seeing the man walking up to the table with a white hat and a white chef's uniform on, I am shocked when I realize it is David. He looks at me like he saw a ghost. Embarrassed, I immediately put my head down.

Sebay says, "We both would like to thank you for a great meal."

David looks down at me like he wants to put his hands around my neck and strangle me.

By now I'm ready to get off this yacht, but we are far away from the shore. Slowly, I bring my head up and say, "Yes, that was a great meal."

David looks at me and then pauses before saying, "Thanks. Uh, Mr. Sebay, do you need me for anything else."

"No, that will be all," Sebay nods gratefully.

Avoiding my eyes, David excuses himself. "I will be downstairs if you need me for anything else."

As he is walking away, he turns around and flashes me a look of disgust. The rest of the time I am on the yacht, David makes himself scarce. An hour, or so has passed and the captain comes to the table.

"Are you too ready to jet ski?" He asks.

"Yes, we are about to go change," Sebay tells him.

"Okay," the captain says. "I'll drop both jet skis in the water."

Sebay shows me where I can go to change. Immediately, David starts interrogating me once I'm downstairs.

"What are you doing with this guy?"

"Keep your voice down. This is a business meeting."

"I don't know of any business meeting that takes place between a man and woman on a yacht. We have to talk."

"Not right now. Later."

"Yeah, because you have a lot of explaining to do."

Rushing into the bathroom, I wash off all my makeup and put my hair back in a ponytail. After putting on my skimpy, two-piece bikini that shows all my curves, I saunter back upstairs. Sebay is sitting down listening to the band play music and drinking a Bahama Mama. As I'm walking towards Sebay, he stands. "You are so beautiful."

"Thank you."

"Come on baby, let's get wet." He flashes a sly grin my way as I register the double meaning of his words.

I'd love to get wet with him and I wasn't talking about in the ocean. I'm checking him out and can't help but notice his nice, round butt. He is built and has ripped muscles, proving that he has almost no fat on his body. Standing next to him, I can't help but rub one of biceps.

"Wow, you must work out a lot."

"Yeah, but I would love to work out with you baby."

"Mmm, that sounds good." I give him a sexy glance.

130

"Hmm, don't get me started." We share a laugh.

By now we are staring each other down in longing. Suddenly, I hear the captain say, "The jet skis are waiting for you two." He gives us both a life jacket. We get on the jet skis and the first thing we do is race. By my surprise, I won. Something told me he let me win.

After an hour on the jet skis, I ask, "Have you had enough yet?"

Sebay looks at me as he squints his eyes from the sun, "Yes, I'm ready to go back to the boat. It's hot out here."

Racing back to the boat, he put the pedal to the metal. That time Sebay won. He throws his arms up in victory. "I'm the winner, so what do I get?" He has a big smile on his face. "That'll be a surprise for another time Sebay."

"Don't be scared Dunja," he says to me and licks his sexy lips. He is so enticing.

"Whatever," I giggle.

By the time we get back on the yacht it's five o' clock.

"Let's go look at that property you liked," I say getting us back on the track of business.

"Yeah, you're right. I've been having so much fun, I totally forgot about that," he admits. As attracted as I am to him, I want to get to the money.

"You will love this office property. I've got the perfect spot for you and it's not far from this dock."

After freshening up, I redo my makeup and change into a pretty pink and white dress. To complete my look, I have a pink purse and white four-inch heels. Men love to see women in shoes like that. Truth be told my feet be killing me. It's a job to look good and beauty is pain. I'm hoping I don't see David. He is so pissed off at me and will probably never speak to me again.

Removing my contacts, I put my glasses on. Going for a more business look, I want Sebay to take me seriously when I try to sell him this commercial property.

"Well, look at Ms. Businesswoman," Sebay says when he lays eyes on me.

"You look very nice too." Sebay looks like he just stepped out of a Rolls-Royce. He definitely has that rich and famous swag. Taking my hand, he leads me off the boat.

"You can follow me. I'll text you the address. That way you can put it in your navigational GPS in case we get separated."

"Cool," he agrees.

We get in our cars and drive off.

He was very specific about the type of commercial property he wants. It has to be able to hold at least a capacity of seven hundred employees. His profile stated that his company is moving from Los Angeles, California to Houston, Texas.

In his email he let me know that he would be spending a lot of time in his office, so it should be comfortable and the ambience must make him feel like he's at home. We both get out of our cars and meet up in front of the building. He stops and says, "You found me the perfect place Dunja. Plus, I like this neighborhood."

We both walk into the building and go up to the fifteenth floor, where his personal office will be. Putting a lot of attention into this project, I asked Rose to furnish the office building a little.

Rose did a fantastic job and I am thinking about giving her a bonus.

His eyes gleam as he takes it all in. "I like the fact that you thought about furnishing it. It gives me more of a homey feeling."

We start walking down a long hallway, and off to the right is a room. "I saved the best for last."

We walk into the room and I immediately lock the door behind us. Sebay really looks impressed at that point. "Dunja, you really know my tastes. This is excellent."

After he pulls me into a hug, things get intense. His big, strong hands suddenly cuff my butt cheeks.

"I want you," he says breathlessly.

And the next thing you know, we are literally ripping each other's clothes off. Mmm, that man can kiss. When I say that he has a skillful tongue, I'm not lying. It is all over me. My neck, my breasts and my thighs. Then his hands are in my scalp, pulling my hair as he feeds me his sweet tongue again.

"Sebay… baby… ohh… myyyy…"

He enters me slowly and fills me to capacity. He's packing way more than David.

"Dunja… you feel amazing… mmm…" His hands gripped my waist as he took me on the ride of my life.

Our legs are entangled as our bodies do a sinful tango. In no time we are both lost in the throes of pleasure, thrusting and gyrating our bodies frantically.

"What are you doing to me?" Screaming out, I just can't contain myself.

Sebay is filling my depths like no other man I've ever been with. The feeling of my G-spot quivering made my entire body spasm. The sensation must've sent him over the edge. He clutched my hips and grinded upward.

"Argghhh… Dunja… I'm cuming baby!"

Collapsing on my chest, he is breathing all hard. We are both spent and just lay there on the cool floor trying to catch our breath. The sound of his phone ringing spoils the moment. I can hear a woman yelling at him. She is saying that dinner's been waiting for him for an hour. She asks if he's on his way?

"Yes, I'm wrapping up my meeting."

Yeah right. More like wrapping his legs around me. After he ends his call, my cell phone rings. It's the sound of sirens letting me know it's Reece.

"What you doing, baby girl? I thought you said you was going to call me back."

Rolling my eyes in annoyance, I say, "I'm not done with my meeting, so let me get back with you."

He sounds disappointed. "It's all good. Holla back."

Sebay and I decide to get up and go, because both of our phones are ringing off the hook. He gives me a deep kiss and hugs me before we go outside.

"I'll call you tomorrow with a decision about buying the commercial property. Do you have the contract with you?"

"Yes." Reaching in my briefcase, I give him the paperwork.

He says, "I will have my attorney look over everything. I had a great time."

"Me too."

He walks me to my car and opens the door just like a gentleman.

"Maybe we can get together again soon."

"Maybe." With that said, I get in my car and drive off.

My phone rings early the next morning.

"Hello."

"I can't get you out of my mind. I haven't had so much fun in a long time."

It is Sebay. "Me either. I had a great time."

"If you don't have anything planned, maybe we can see each again and do a repeat. I also want to buy the property. My attorney and I can be at your office tomorrow at ten. Will that work for you?"

"That's perfect." Doing a fist pump, I realize that my cooch had put in the work.

Immediately calling Rose after we hang up, I let her know we had a closing the next day. "Mr. Sebay will be buying the property in clear Lake City," I announce excitedly.

She says, "Great, Ms Dunja. You've been working very hard to close on that deal."

"Thank you Rose. Make sure you order breakfast in the morning."

With a smile, Rose says cordially, "I'll take care of it."

"Thank you and have a good night."

"No problem and you do the same Ms. Dunja."

When I get home, I take a shower and pass out on my California King sized bed. The fresh air that blew off the lake into my opened window makes me sleep peacefully.

My alarm goes off at five am. It's a very important day for me. Once I close on the property I will get a nice commission check.

After a long, hot shower, I get extra cute, because I'm meeting with Sebay and his attorney. Grabbing my purse, I make my way to my truck and hit the gas. I get to work at nine am. Rose is already in the office.

"What time did you get here?" I ask her when I walk inside.

Her response is, "Seven."

"Well, good morning and how are you doing?"

"Good morning boss lady. I'm great. Thank you for asking. How's your mother?"

"She's doing well. Is everything ready for the closing?"

"Yes," she confirms. "Your hot cappuccino is waiting for you in the conference room."

Walking into the conference room, I notice Luke, my attorney is there.

"Good morning, Ms. Dunja."

"Good morning Luke."

Grabbing my cappuccino, I take a seat. Less than forty-five minutes later, a man enters the room. He shakes my hand and says, "Hi Ms. Dunja, I'm Mr. Sebay's attorney, Mr. Paul Jackson." Both attorneys thank me for breakfast. A few minutes later, Rose walks Mr. Sebay into the conference room. We both look at each-other like we might act unprofessional later.

"Good morning, Ms. Dunja."

"Good morning, Mr. Sebay."

It's hard to hold back my feelings. He looks at me and winks his eye, but nobody sees it other than me. The closing goes great. When it's complete, everyone cordially shakes hands. All I can think about is my commission check. Mother will be proud of me following in her footsteps. Giving the key to Mr. Sebay, I thank him for closing with my company. "You'll find a gift at your office."

"What is it?" His eyes narrow sexily as he asks.

"I'm not telling, but it is from Tiffany's."

Looking at me, he smiles. "Thank you Ms. Dunja."

Everybody has left already, except for Sebay. With his eyes still glued to me, he says, "I would love to see you this evening. Do you have any time for me?"

Nope, being that I had his money, I don't need him now. That's when I lie and say, "I'm not feeling well. I'm going to go home early to get some rest. Can I take a rain check?"

By now he's holding my hand. He kisses it. "I'm sorry you're under the weather." That's when I call Rose into the conference room. "I'm not feeling well Rose, so I'm going home early." Rose knows that is my sign to give him the boot out the door. She picks up quickly. "Well, Mr. Sebay, guess we are closing the office now. I'll walk you to the door, before I lock up."

Glancing back on his way to the door, he says, "Dunja, I hope you feel better."

"Thank you Rose. I thought he'd never leave."

Laughing, she jokes, "Ms. Dunja, I don't know how you keep your men in line. One day it's going to catch up to you."

"Not today baby." We both laugh at that and say our goodbyes.

Just in case Sebay is stalking me outside, I take the back exit.

When I get home, I call Rose to let her know I will not be coming into the office until eleven the next morning. I needed to sleep in. She understands and says, "Ms. Dunja be working very hard. And like you say, Ms.Dunja, it's hard out here be for a pimp."

That's a good laugh. "By the way, you can have the day off."

"Oh, thank you so much Ms. Dunja!"

"No problem. Enjoy your weekend. See you Monday."

Deciding not to dress up, I get out of the bed, shower and just throw on some jeans and a t-shirt. Instead of cooking breakfast, I decide to grab something on my way to work. Stopping at Chick-Fil-A, I grab a chicken sandwich and gets to the office right at eleven o'clock. Two hours pass by and I am ready to go home. All my sexual escapades are catching up with me. It has been a long week, so I decide to close the office. When I get home, I immediately power off my phone. I didn't want to hear from anyone, until Saturday morning. Taking a nice, hot bubble bath, I have my candles, wine, and soft music playing. Feeling myself drifting off to sleep in the tub, I decide to get my butt out before I drown.

Climbing in bed, I watch the news until I fall asleep. The next morning, I wake up refreshed and power my phone back on. There are like fifteen messages. Five are from Sebay, five are from David and the other five are from Reece.

Not bothering to call either Sebay, or David back, I decide to call Reece. David is ranting and raving on all his messages. Who does he think he's talking to? He was definitely not talking to me. Sebay is just begging, wanting some of my kitty cat. It was good and all, but after getting his money, I didn't need anything else from him.

Reese mentions food when I call him and says he'll pick me up at three. At least I don't have to cook today. He wants to take me to a family BBQ at the park around the corner from his Aunt Frances' house. When I call him back, he picks up on the first ring. Anxious much?

"I have been trying to call you all morning," he says instead of hello.

These men are testing my patience, because I haven't committed to anybody. "You got me now baby. I got your message."

"You gonna be ready on time?" He sounds mighty damn bossy.

"Yes, I'll be ready," I tell him instead of cussing him out. Getting up, I fix a quick breakfast, wishing I hadn't pissed David off. He would've been there to make me breakfast in bed. After a quick shower, I dressed casually. Then I put on my big loop earrings and a cute pair of sandals. My doorbell rings and I look out of the peephole. It is Reece of course. He's chocolate, tall, with deep dimples, and a clean-cut look.

When I swing the door open, Reece is staring at me like I'm a snack. "Girl, you know how to put them threads together. You lookin' good."

Blushing, I say, "Thank you boo."

Although I am a professional woman, I love myself some hood men. You can be a good girl, but sometimes you just want a little nasty in your life. Nothing's wrong with that, especially if he knows how to work it. One thing about me is, I don't mind giving hood dudes their props. They don't mind putting it down and getting down-right nasty in the bedroom.

Pulling up to the park, I haven't seen so many bad little kids running around in my life. We get out of the car and Reece introduces me to his Aunt Frances. She seems really nice. "Baby, gone over there and get yourself some food. Don't be scared." She points over to the delicious looking spread of food. Reece and I make our way over to the food. Dang, his folks know how to throw down. There are ribs, chicken, corn on the cob, potato salad, coleslaw, deviled eggs, baked beans, sweet potato pie, red velvet cake, and my favorite, peach cobbler. We sit down at a picnic table and he introduces me to his first cousins Marvin, Roxanne, James Jr., Darrel and Thomas.

All of them are cordial and make me feel very welcome. Music is playing, and everybody is playing dominoes and spades. Off to the side, the younger generation is shooting dice. They are yelling and screaming, and two of his cousins start to fight each other, saying the other is cheating.

That's when an older gentleman walks over to them and says, "Shut it down. They break it up pretty quickly, so I figured nobody messed with him. Then it is announced that there will be a game of softball and anybody could play.

Reece looks over at me, "You wanna play? You know what, never mind. You too cute to play. You can't break a nail, because then I'll have to pay for you to get them done."

With a giggle, I agree, "You're right about that boo."

He chuckles. "Let's go watch them play."

After a couple hours, I tell Reece we should go. It's getting late and I need to get ready to go to the club later.

"Okay baby, let's go say bye to Aunt Frances."

I thank his Aunt for having me and we leave.

We pull up in front of my house. "Can I come in?" His eyes are anxious.

"Yes boo."

We walk in my house and before I can close the door, he picks me up and carries me upstairs to the bedroom. Then, he slowly starts to undress me, one piece at a time. Once I am butt naked, I remove his clothes. We are passionately kissing each other, but I abruptly pull away. As I walk away to the bathroom, I sexily gesture for him to follow me. We jump in the shower and he lathers body wash onto my sponge, then he proceeds to wash me down.

Oh yeah, I'm turned on when he makes sure my kitty cat is all nice and clean. When he is done washing my body he is ready. When I tell you, this man put it on me. The hood side came out of him for real. It is like he has popped a couple Viagra, although he doesn't need any.

"Reece… uhhh…" Holding on to him, I scratch his back as he goes deep.

The way he's grinding inside of me like a male stripper is taking me there.

"You feel that?" He asks with his warm, soft lips on my neck.

"Every inch," I breath, making sure I throw it back at him with each stroke.

In no time, we are at the peak of pleasure at the same time.

"Yessss!!!" As I scream, he lets out a loud grunt letting me know we are coming together.

Getting out of the shower, we dry each other off and lie down on my bed to cuddle for a short while.

"You have to go now baby," I tell Reese. "I need my beauty sleep before the club tonight."

"Baby girl, that's cool. I already had you climbing the walls and screaming my name."

"So, you got jokes." Laughing, I stand on my tiptoes to give him a sweet kiss. After locking the door behind him, I climb back in my bed and go to sleep with no problem. If anything, there's a smile on my face. My power nap ends at seven. With a yawn, I get out of bed and get ready. My dress is a tight, black bondage dress that is short and sexy. The women are going to hate, but I'm sure the men will want to buy me drinks and dance with me all night.

While I'm driving to the club my phone rings. It is my mother calling from overseas.

"Hi sweetheart, how are you doing?"

"I'm great mother. On my way out to the club with the girls."

"How are the divas?"

"They're all fine."

"Well, dear, I'm calling to let you know that I will be in the States in two days."

"Lovely, we can shop until we drop. You'll be very proud of me. I just closed a huge deal and got a big commission this week."

"Great honey, we can catch up on everything on Monday. I'll let you go Dunja. We'll talk later. Be safe."

"Wait, mother, take down Rose's email address and send her your itinerary. She'll have my driver pick you up on Monday from the airport."

"Will do. Kisses Dunja."

"Kisses."

At ten pm, I pull up at the club. My girls are getting valet just in time. Once we are out of our cars, we hug and air kiss.

"Are you ladies ready to party?" I ask them.

One of the divas spat, "I didn't get dressed up for nothing."

All of us laugh and agree to that. Anytime that we walk into a club, we get so much attention. We go straight over to the VIP lounge.

Reece walks over to greet us. "You ladies are all looking hot as fish grease."

Laughing, we thank him in unison.

"Well ladies, everything is all set up and ready for you," Reece says, pointing at our VIP table.

The music is bumping from the speakers, making us all have to shout to communicate.

"Let's dance baby," Reece suggests taking my hand. "We have fifteen minutes before my shift starts." He works in the club as a bouncer.

We dance close until he has to go.

"I'll check up on you, later. Order whatever you want, including food and drinks. I'll cover the tab."

"I have no problem at all with that."

As soon as he leaves the table men are coming offering to spend their coins on us.

One of my girls say, "Whatever you do, don't break up with Reece."

Rolling my eyes, I retort, "You don't know what I go through with him."

Another one chimes in, "Don't mess it up for us."

Not believing those hoes, I look at them, and ask, "Really?"

They laugh it off and we all decide to get on the dance floor and dance. We are lit and have so much fun twerking and dancing up on those fine men up in there.

We leave the dance floor after getting all sweaty and go order all kinds of food and drinks. After we get full we are tired and ready to go. Reece returns to the table to check up on us.

"It's time for us to roll out bae," I inform him with a yawn. "I'm tired."

He suggests, "Why don't you just wait a little while longer. The club doesn't close 'til four. Then I can go home with you."

"I'm stayin' with one of my divas tonight. We are goin' to church in the morning." Lord forgive me for telling that little white lie.

His eyes cast down in disappointment. "Well, I'll call you tomorrow."

"That's cool." By now my feet are killing me. The cute look is off my and face all I want is to go home, take a shower and go to sleep.

After saying my good nights to all the divas, we head on home. The first thing I do is rush to wash the sweat off me and then I hit the sheets. When I wake up the next morning there is a message from Sebay. He wants to come over and put me to sleep. That man's about to really piss me off really. My ass is not in the mood for a booty call. Rose left a voice message letting me know that she got the email from my mother and would keep me informed.

Because it is Sunday, I decide not to bother Rose. Sending her a text back, I let her know I'd received her message.

On Monday I am up by five in the morning. I'd cleaned up the house from top to bottom the night before, because mother is coming. After a refreshing shower, I do my hair, put my makeup on and throw on a gray power suit. Then I am and out the door and on my way to the office. Of course, Rose has my cappuccino hot and ready when I get there.

"Here's your mother's itinerary. She will be landing at one." Rose adds, "I ordered lunch for you two."

My mother's flight is on time. The driver picks her up and drops her off at my office. Trying to handle all the business I can before my mother starts talking to me, I try reaching one of my clients to only get the voicemail. My mother walks through the door and greets me with a hug.

"Hello darling.

My client calls back and I transfer him over to Rose to make an appointment.

"How was your flight mother?"

She says, "Long, but it's always nice flying first class. It makes it a little better. Do you plan on working all day?"

"No mother, I just need to sign this paperwork and then we can eat the lunch Rose ordered."

Mother and I work on a project together after lunch. By four, I tell Rose we are leaving for the day.

"Should I forward all your calls to your cell phone?"

"No. I don't want to be bothered while mother's in town."

"Will do Ms. Dunja."

Our next destination is the shopping mall. There's nothing like retail therapy.

Mother and I catch up on everything while we shop. I fill her in on my big client and the big commission I got last week. She tells me she is very proud of me.

"Look at you, following in your mother's footsteps," she beams at me.

Deciding not to talk to any of my men, I want to spend some quality time with my mother and that's what I did. During the entire week, I don't return any of their calls.

Mother left on Sunday afternoon.

"I won't be back for a while, so keep up the great work. I love you."

"I love you too." Mother adds, "Dunja, I'm going to tell you who your father is. He was the president of the United States at the time I got pregnant. He made me promise that I would never tell you who he is. Part of me keeping silent afforded us a great life. He paid for our house and my business. Dunja, you have the best education in the world because of him, so I stayed silent. The main reason was because he is married."

By now I cannot stop crying. Mother says, "I never wanted you to know, but I think it's important that you know now."

Never understanding the reason for her waiting so long to tell me, I decide not to speak on it.

"He said I could only tell you who he is when he died. That is why I came into town. One of his Secret Service agents called me and told me that he wanted me to be at his funeral."

After she revealed his name, she left.

Pacing the floor of my office, I can't help but cry. Rose rushes in. She finds me passed out with my cell phone in my hand. Rose picks up the phone and tells my mother she will call her back, because I am out cold. Ross starts to call 911 just as I come to.

"I'm fine Rose. Call my mother back and let her know that I'm okay."

From that point on, I stop speaking to my mother. She's been very successful at dogging men out. Not wanting to be like her, I didn't date for about five months. Then I decided to only date one man.

Are you wondering what ever happened to the men I dogged out? Sebay would send me flowers every day and I got so tired of sending them back. Then one day, out of the blue, they stopped.

Not long after that, I saw on the news that Sebay had got into a boating accident and died. David was so persistent, I had to block his number. He was blowing me up all times of the day. He would leave nasty messages on my voicemail and fill up my inbox, so no one else could leave a message. Of course, I never returned his calls. One of my divas told me that he ended up being a top chef at an expensive five-star hotel.

Reece kept coming up to my job and saying he wouldn't leave until I talked to him. All I did was put my security on him.

That's the only way you can get rid of a brother from the hood. You know they did not play about going to jail. The divas were mad at me, because we had to find another club to go to. There was no more VIP. Reece ended up getting married and I never heard from him again.

After I gave Rose her bonus, she got her real estate license and started her own business.

This is the daily quote for the day. By Ms. Kim McCall If you think the grass is greener on the other side, think again. If you don't want to get dogged out stop running around looking for pussycats! Meow! The story behind this chapter is, if you get someone that treats you right and they have your back, stick with them.

THE CHASE OF FUGITIVES

On this day, I find myself waking up crying and remembering my mother. She passed away at an early age. My brother and I had to move in with our grandma, Vanetta. It is a nice spring day and my brother Tafari is just coming in from work. I can hear him moving around downstairs. He works nights as a bartender at an upscale night club named *21 and Over*. He gets up every morning around nine to go to the studio and lay down tracks. My brother has been working very hard to finish production on his album and music video. Then, he comes home and takes a two-hour power nap before his night shift at the club. Tafari recently met this cool promoter that is assisting him with marketing.

Tafari has been saving money for the past six months to complete this project. He doesn't know it, but he's in the perfect industry; bartending. The club manager told him that once his album and music video are complete, he is welcome to perform live at the club. We are both excited about that. It is so dope to have an up and coming rapper in the family. My brother just needs one more investor. Our uncle told us that a popular speaker is hosting a two-day conference at our church that will teach us how to make some extra money. My brother and grandma are really interested in going to the conference. He thinks he's going to be able to flip the money he saved to make more money.

My name is Nyla and I'm a professional bounty hunter. Bail bondsmen call me to find and capture fugitives in exchange for a monetary reward. I typically get a percentage of the bail. The compensation is worth the risks.

It's such a hard task trying to get ready for church. My uncle LaMarcus is the Senior Pastor and my aunt Leticia holds down her first lady spot. "Helping Hands Kingdom" is considered one of the mega churches here in Phoenix, AZ. Robert and Kathy will be giving the *Helping Hands Kingdom* congregation a presentation on how we can buy stocks and bonds from their company at a low rate and get a nice return in our pockets. My uncle LaMarcus knows both speakers very well, because they went to college together. He speaks very highly of them, so the program must be legit. There's no way I can miss an opportunity to learn how to make more money.

As the aroma of bacon floats upstairs, my mouth waters for grandma's traditional breakfast of eggs, biscuits and grits. I'm starving and can't wait to eat. The next thing I hear is my brother Tafari, knocking on my door, "Sis are you up yet?"

He gets on my nerves with that. "Yes, I'm getting ready to take a shower. I'll be down in few."

Getting out of the bed, I jump in the shower. There's not much I have to do with my hair. It's naturally curly, so I just wet it and go. My brother and I have never been close to our father's side of the family. He passed away when I was five and Tafari was two years old. We were told by my grandma that our father was a police officer. He was killed in the line of duty. I believe that genes are very powerful and must be the reason I am following in his footsteps. I feel honored to be carrying on the family legacy. The best thing about my job other than capturing fugitives is the money. One thing about me is, I love getting those coins. The steel box in my closet was where I keep my hand gun. It is always locked and loaded.

Choosing a pair of black slacks and a blue button-down shirt, I strap my gun in the holster and hurry downstairs to eat. You're probably wondering why I carry a gun inside the house? As a bounty hunter, it's best to always be strapped. My gun goes to church, Disney World and the bathroom. Wherever I go, it goes.

Tafari just stares at me with that smirk he always gives. "Thought you would never get out of that shower."

"Beauty takes time." I say with a chuckle as, I stroke my hair. "It can't be rushed." He just flashes a gap toothed smile my way. "You got jokes."

My grandma asks one of us to pray over the food.

Speaking up, I agree to do it. All three of us hold hands and pray. My grandma is a very religious person and the backbone of our small family. As always, she outdid herself. The food is great, but it's almost time for the financial seminar and we are all eager. Grandma is even more eager than us. "Baby, if they can show us how to make money, we'll be good honey."

Tafari and I both start laughing. "Let's go grandma!" I beckon.

As we pull up to the church, I realize that we should've left earlier. There are hardly any parking spaces, but thank goodness for the little shuttles. I hold things down very well as head of security. Yeah, I wasn't just a bounty hunter. As we make our way inside the church, the choir is singing in beautiful harmony. Every time I hear the choir, it makes me emotional. It's hard to hold back my tears, but I must always maintain a tough persona, because of my job. The choir takes a break after belting out three uplifting songs. The announcements for the week are read after that. My uncle LaMarcus strolls up the podium.

"Do we have any first-time visitors here with us today?" He looks out into the crowd.

Today there are five new visitors and he thanks them graciously for coming. As customary, the first lady walks up to give a speech. She welcomes the visitors and tells them she really appreciates them. She then asks them to fill out a visitor's card and turn it in at the bookstore.

"The pastor and I have a special gift just for you." She encourages us to mingle among one another. You can hear the song "Happy" playing lightly in the background. That's why I love my church. It is such a home away from home, although the congregation is large. My uncle LaMarcus returns to the podium and conducts offering, followed by a shockingly brief thirty-minute sermon. That's unheard of. My uncle is almost always long-winded. He states that he wants to save the rest of the service for his special guests.

Robert Stockholm, a tall, adorable-looking, red-headed man with square, wire framed glasses stood up. He is accompanied by his wife, Kathy. She is thin and short with blond hair that's done in a pixie cut. She kind of reminds me of the actress Jennifer Lawrence. They didn't look like they belong together, but it is obvious they are in love. My uncle briefly explains that he and Robert played football together. Robert met his wife when they were in college and she was working part-time in the cafeteria.

"I guess eating all that red velvet cake equaled love-at-first-sight," my uncle jokes. The whole congregation is in an uproar of laughter. Then, my uncle changes the subject. "Have you ever wondered what your life could be like if you had more money in your pocket? My good friends will be talking to you about stocks and bonds today. If you want to save for retirement, your children's college fund, or a raising a family, you'll learn how to better save after this presentation. Please give a round of applause for Robert and Kathy Stockholm!"

Robert allows his wife to speak first. "I'm very excited to be here. Thank you for having us! Your pastor is a wonderful, selfless man and I'm honored to call him my friend." Kathy whispers something in her husband's ear and he proceeds towards the podium. "Thank you again for having us. I'm going to share a little about our company, Stockholm Financial. We can manage your personal portfolio if you decide to buy into our stocks and bonds. I guarantee I can double your investment in six months."

Everyone is glued to the presentation. A lot of people are oohing and ahhing. My grandma and my brother are sitting in the row in front of me. My brother is the first one to say, "I'm going to sign up."

Then, my grandma piggybacks. "Sounds good to me." However, I'm the sensible one. It takes me a little longer to know if I'm going to give up my money.

Working too hard to get my money, I pray it's legit. Robert is too cute though with deep dimples and nice, bedroom eyes.

Lord, forgive me! It's been a minute since I've had good sex with a man. My river is overflowing due to my crazy schedule. That's when I start to daydream about this fine guy that I work with. He always makes small talk and smiles at me. He is so fine! I hope he will eventually ask me out, but he hasn't yet. Oh well! It's not good to mix business with pleasure anyway. Besides, I am in church. Back to reality.

Robert smiles and talks into the mic. "Thank you all for your time." Then, he directs the congregation to the sign-up sheet in the lobby and welcomes us back for an additional seminar the following week. Once the pastor dismisses us, everyone runs out of the sanctuary. They are scurrying fast like little roaches to sign up. I'm staring at Robert like he is the only glass of water in the Sahara Desert. The thirst is too real. The need to have my back banged out is crucial. Hey, I'm even thinking about it in a church. That is how serious it is. Even Tafari peeps me and calls me out on it. "Sis, you look thirsty."

All I can do is laugh at him for knowing me like he does.

Lord, forgive me for the little white lie I'm about to tell my brother. "No, Tafari…I just feel so hot. Ain't you hot too?"

Man, I would love to strip Robert down and see what he is working with. Is it a mere three inches, or maybe six? My eyes are steadily glued to his pants. From where I'm standing, he's got to be at least six inches. Snapping back into reality, I can hear my grandma whining about leaving. It's obvious that she's going to sign-up for the next seminar. I can see it in her eyes.

My brother mentions that he hopes his six months of savings can double from purchasing the stock. Suddenly, my cell phone rings. It is my partner texting me directions. He states that he thinks he's found Tracy Greenbrae. We had been tracking her for a while. Now, it's action time. I'm ready to get that woman. After my goodbyes to Tafari and grandma, I drive off. It doesn't take me long to get to the location. Once I pull up, my partner greets me.

"She's inside the grocery store. A cashier told me she's here every Sunday."

As soon as he said that, Tracy walks out with bags in her hand.

"Walk up to her cautiously," he advised.

By the time I reach her, she drops her groceries and starts to run. It is a good thing I put on some tennis shoes, because I took off after her. My partner jumps in his vehicle and starts to follow me. When we catch up to her, I tackle her like I'm a football player. Then, out of the blue, this dumb girl starts fighting me. Instead of keeping it procedure, I go crazy on her. My fists connect with her mouth and blood shoots out. She has the nerve to pull my hair and try to bite me. The struggle finally ends and I am able to handcuff her. We take her to jail and I notice she has a few bruises, but nobody says anything. We fill out all the necessary paperwork and head out.

"We're getting a fat check for this one!" My partner pats my head jokingly. "You almost lost your *long,* black hair."

"Well, I am about to go home with all these beautiful, silky strands. I'm so tired."

The next day is my day off and all I want to do is sleep. My face and ears grimace at the sound of grandma's voice. She is yelling upstairs.

"Hey, Nyla do you want to eat with me!"

"No, thank you. I'll eat later!" Finally, I get out of bed and go take a shower. After that I get back in the bed, wet and all. It is my day off. On my way downstairs, I go to look for my brother. My grandma tells me that he already left for the studio.

"He'll be back in a couple hours. Come sit with me." She immediately starts making small talk and then asks, "Are you going to buy any stock from Robert and Kathy?"

"I'm not quite sure. Thank you for the food grandma." After cleaning up the kitchen, I go back to bed.

Taking a short power nap, I have a freaky dream and it is about Robert. I am sitting down in a chair and he's pouring honey all over my body. He licks every ounce off with long, warm tongue and it feels so real. Then he starts exploring my inner depths with his long, agile fingers. Ohh… I can feel myself about to…

Suddenly, I hear banging at my bedroom door. "Just checking on you, sis!"

Snapping out of my dream, I notice my nipples are super hard and I'm tingling between my thighs. What a dream. Getting out of bed, I scramble around to find some clothes to throw on. Swinging the door open, I'm wearing my best stank face. Tafari starts laughing at me. "Old habits are hard to break, huh sis? Did you have to find something to put on before you could answer the door?" My brother teases me further. "Sis, one day the house will catch on fire and because you hate wearing clothes to bed, you will be giving the firefighters a live nude show."

Rolling my eyes at him, I say, "Whatever bro. What do you want?"

"Nothin' sis...I'm just being nosy." He chuckles. "Did you catch the girl you were tracking?"

Of course, I have to brag to Tafari. "Yup and you know I'm getting a big fat check because of it."

He gives me a high-five. "That's what up, sis! Are you going to buy into that stock on Saturday?"

Not sure why everybody is trying to get me to buy into Robert and Kathy's stock, I let out a sigh. I have stock in my own job. My money doesn't flow like that. "Bro, I'm just not sure. Can you respect that?"

Tafari began to throw imaginary money in the air. "Grandma and I are about to make it rain after we put our money in on Saturday."

Throwing a pillow at him, I say, "Good for you! Now, get out of my room. I'm going back to sleep!"

When I wake up it's early Wednesday morning. Having to rush out the door again without breakfast, I tell my grandma that she does not have to cook for me. I am going to treat myself to Waffle House today. The next day is a repeat of the day before. This goes on for four days and before I know it, it is Saturday morning. It is difficult to drag myself out of bed. My cell phone vibrates on my nightstand. It is my squad leader.

"Nyla, how are you doing?" He asks.

Here we go again. I know what's coming next. "Sir, I've been working all kinds of crazy hours trying to get this promotion. Hard work indeed pays off."

My squad leader breathes a heavy sigh. "We're shorthanded and could use your help with this special project."

Why do they not let me breathe? And on a Saturday.

"You do not have to go into the field. I only need you to help with the paperwork for a sting that we are doing on Monday." Basically, this man just *told* me instead of asking. I'm not very happy about that and I have my heart set on going to the seminar the next day. My body and mind are both eager to view the fine man that is Robert! Damn! Thanks to my boss that wet dream is over. Geesh, he is a pain in my ass. However, the boss gets what the boss wants and into work I go. Once again, I jump out of my bed, took a shower, say goodbye to my brother and my grandma, and off I go.

When I get back an hour later, I tell Tafari and grandma that I am going to cook breakfast. Grandma gives me a blank stare.

"Well, maybe I need to fall out of my seat."

Giving grandma one of my famous pouty faces, I say, "Grandma, you're so cute and you got jokes. I just love you. Now, what would you like to eat?"

Are grandmas naturally slow? It's like they take a gazillion seconds just to answer a simple question. "Nyla baby, I'll take some grits, some biscuits, pork sausage and a scrambled egg. Now, use the egg whites…Grandma has to watch her cholesterol." After pouring her a tall glass of orange juice, I proceed with preparing our meal. After we finish eating, I clean the kitchen and let everyone know that it is time to get dressed for the seminar. Never have I been so excited to go to a conference. It is just because I want to see that sexy ass Robert. His wife never even crosses my mind.

When we arrive at the church, it looks like half the congregation is already there. A mass email was sent out inviting everyone to come out. My uncle reintroduced Robert and Kathy as his college friends, because some people were not at church last Sunday.

Robert and Kathy step up to the podium and start speaking. They have brought twenty of their employees there to help. We watch a fifteen-minute presentation with their shareholders giving personal testimonies about how they acquired such large checks. They brag about how they are living it up with the extra income, taking vacations, and buying luxury cars. Three couples state that they have enough money to put down on a new house. After the end of the presentation, Robert hypes up the crowd further. "Now who's ready to make this money? Let me see by a show of hands. My employees are outside in the lobby waiting on you to sign up, so get up and start your future!" Everybody stands and makes their way out to the lobby. Also, I notice some people leaving. Grandma isn't swayed by any of the naysayers.

"Grandson, guess they don't wanna double their money, but you and I will." That's when my uncle comes over. "Mother, how much are you going to invest in Robert's stock?" LaMarcus questions. Grandma loves her son, but she is not going to tolerate his disrespect. Grandma looks Uncle LaMarcus square in the eye. "I can handle my own finances. Mind your business. You'll live longer." Grandma chuckles, but I think she hit a soft spot.

My uncle just turns around and walks off. The sound of my uncle mumbling made me kind of sad. He probably is mumbling about how hard his daddy worked to save money for retirement. His mother is set for life and he prays she doesn't use it all. Now, it is my grandma's turn in line. She pulls a checkbook out and writes a check for three thousand dollars. For some reason, I thought I heard her say ten thousand dollars. It's best to just let my grandma do her, because I didn't want her arguing with me. They assign her a personal account number after her payment has been made. The employee then advises her that they will send her a monthly newsletter and quarterly report via email.

"This investment is very important to me. I hope the return on my money will pay for studio time and for me to finish my album. I'm an up and coming rapper," Tafari tells one of the employees.

The man just shrugs his shoulders as if he's not interested and continues processing his application. The man informs Tafari,

"The application fee is fifty dollars. You have the option to pay by cash, debit, credit or check."

Tafari passes him a thousand dollars in cash.

On our way back home, we are making small talk. Grandma is too excited to have her money doubled. Tafari is just staring into space, drooling with a huge cheesy grin. Grandma pats him on the hand and he snaps out of his daydream. "Grandson, when will your album be finished?"

Tafari's eyes are still lit from his daydream. "Three months, grandma." He spoke confidently. "Now remember, you said you'll come and watch me perform."

"Yes, grandson, I'll be there for you Tafari."

When we arrive home, no one wants to cook, so grandma puts a pizza in the oven. It is a Canadian bacon and pineapple deep dish pizza.

"I'm going to put to on something comfier. I'll be back." That food is calling my name! We eat, watch a little television and go to bed. My brother and I are working very hard and hustling to save our money. Never did I invest in Robert and Kathy's stock, being that I have stock in the company I work for. For the time being, that is enough.

The next couple months fly by fast. It's early in the week and my alarm is blaring on my nightstand. Not wanting to get up, I just lie there knowing I have to get to the money. Out of nowhere, I hear a loud scream coming from outside. It is grandma. My brother and I leap out of our beds. My first instinct is to grab my gun, so that's what I do. Frantically running down the stairs, I meet my brother at the bottom. Both my brother and I are packing. He has his 357 Magnum and I have my 9mm. We both rush outside to check on grandma.

By the time we reach her, she's not yelling anymore. She's holding two white envelopes in her hand. Waving a green check over her head, she exclaims, "I got my money honey!" With a laugh she gives my brother his envelope.

"For real, grandma? We thought someone was attacking you." I shake my head. Grandma chuckles. "Baby, I'm good! I just can't believe it's only been two months and I got a return."

Maybe I should have invested in Robert and Kathy's stock. My brother and grandma keep bragging about how happy they are. Grandma got a check for six thousand dollars and my brother got a check for three thousand.

"Baby, I must cash this check before the ink dries up," grandma beams proudly.

My brother leaves to go to the studio and grandma and I head to the bank. When we get to the bank, I spot this fine specimen looking me up and down like I'm a snack. Not only does he look good, but he smells even better. I can smell that Usher cologne from a mile away. He is about 6'2, with a mustache and perfectly groomed beard. With that nice pin-stripe Steve Harvey Suit and silk tie, he looks like he just stepped off the cover of GQ magazine. The things that come to mind when I see his firm, hard chest and biceps. Being the woman that I am, I wonder about the size of his package. What was he working with down there? Deciding to strike up a conversation with him, I sashay over and introduce myself. "Hi, how are you? My name is Nyla. Those Stacy Adams you're rocking remind me of a pair my brother has. I love a man with a hot shoe game."

"Thank you, Nyla. You look like you've been working out. Nice calves." With that said, he turns and walks out of the bank. Just like that the conversation ends abruptly. Wow. Not even getting his name, I figure, oh well.

It is now grandma's turn in the line. Watching her sign the check and hand it to the teller, I say, "Grandma, you have all this money, but you do nothing with it. Why don't you splurge a little and take out some money to get your hair and nails done?"

She agrees. "You are right baby girl. I never do anything for myself."

The teller gives grandma her money and we leave. As we are walking to the car, my grandma's cell phone rings. It is Uncle Lamarcus, so she puts him on speaker.

"What are your plans for the day mother?"

"On my way to get beautiful. Going to get my hair and nails done. Would you like to pay for it?" She chuckles but means it.

Turning towards me, she asks, "Nyla baby, can you drop me off at Fanny's shop?"

I nod in agreement.

"Yes, ma'am!"

She picks up where she left off with my uncle. He promises to pick her up when she's all done.

Grandma insists on keeping the phone on the speaker, so the whole world can hear her entire conversation. She refuses to go get a hearing test and it drives all of us crazy. When she is done talking on her cell phone, she places it in her bra. To me that is hilarious. I can relate though. My grandma is such a silly old woman. After dropping her off at the salon, I head to work.

My uncle keeps his word and drops grandma off at home after she's done getting beautified.

For the next month, all Tafari and I do is go to work and come home. It is now the middle of August. Grandma is chillaxing in bed with her feet up, leaning against the cushioned headboard. She's admiring her nails, making a habit of getting them done since I suggested it to her.

"Ms. Ling Ling did a great job!" Grandma declares.

"Oh yes, she did!" I agree admiring her French Manicure.

"Love TKO" blares from her phone's speaker. When did she get that ring tone, I wonder? The phone rings about two more times before she decides to answer. The person on the line is obviously a man.

"Good morning! How are you doing today?"

"I'm fine, but who is this?"

"It's Robert, Ms. Vanetta. I am in the neighborhood and wanted to know if I could stop by to speak with you."

"Well, I don't see why not! We are glad that you came to our church and shared that information on stocks and bonds. Give me a second to get myself together."

"My mother-in-law is with me. I would love for you two to meet."

Grandma gave Robert the address and he tells her he'll see her in twenty minutes. After she hangs up she asks out loud, "I wonder why he wants to come see me?"

* * *

A silver Audi speeds up, then slows down to a crawl. Then it finally comes to a stop, parking at the end of the street. Robert steps out of the car and walks over to the passenger side of the vehicle. There is a woman adjusting a poor excuse for a gray wig, as Richard uses a lot of hand motions while talking to her.

"Now, you remember your lines, right? Your name is Maddie…you're my mother-in-law. Mrs. Vanetta cannot, and I mean cannot know that you are a hot, young blonde. She's old, but not that old," Robert hints. The woman removes the gray wig, shaking it in the air. "Yes, I remember. If she asks me where Kathy is, I'll tell her she's at home preparing lunch. I got this, Robert," she tells him dismissively.

* * *

Ms. Venetta

On my way downstairs, I hear the doorbell ring. This man is very punctual. It's exactly twenty minutes since we spoke. Opening the door, I see Robert and his mother-in-law. Robert hands me a bouquet of yellow roses. "These are beautiful, Robert. I'll find a vase and put them in some water."

Robert points towards the gray-haired woman. "This is my mother-in-law, Ms. Maddie." Simply nodding her head, she waves. She does not come alive until I ask her where Kathy is?

"Oh Kathy, she's at the house, making us a fine lunch. I asked her for egg salad on sourdough bread. I can't wait to get back to eat."

Robert turns, looks at Ms. Maddie and flashes an awkward gaze her way.

"Robert, I must admit that your call took me by surprise today."

Robert clears his throat, while adjusting his necktie. The man exuded such confidence he could convince anyone to buy anything.

"Ms. Vanetta, I just happened to be in the neighborhood and wanted to stop by to see if you're interested in another investment. But, you must do it today. The quarterly reports we send you are positive proof that our company is flourishing."

Not able to stop myself, I am blushing.

"You're right about that Robert. I get my checks on a regular basis."

"What would you say if I am able to offer this special promotion to you? I've only picked out fifteen of my clients to invest and wanted to know if you are interested?"

"You better believe I'm interested. How much do I need to invest?"

Robert takes a deep breath. "For you, only twenty thousand dollars. Again, you must do it today and today only." He sounds so enthusiastic.

"Whoa, that's a lot of money," I hesitate.

If I had like a hundred thousand in the bank that would be easy.

"Your reservations are not unfounded. Just know you will have higher returns if you do this. You will be doubling your money. Trust me." There's a twinkle in his eyes as he talks about money.

"Robert, I don't have a way to get to the bank. Both my grandchildren are at work."

"No problem! I can take you, Ms. Vanetta. We should get going before the bank closes."

We arrive at the bank and they sit down while I wait for my personal banker Mr. Ty. Today is his off day, so they have another teller wait on me.

"Ms. Vanetta, we have a memo to contact your son, Pastor Lamarcus for any amount larger than $1,000. Ah, but I also see another memo saying that Mr. Ty overruled that and took it off. Is that true, Mrs. Vanetta?"

Nodding my head in agreement, I say, "Yes, that's true. It is my money and I do what I want to do with it." "You do know that by withdrawing $20,000, it is going to put a second mortgage on your house. You must have this paid back within three months. There is a very high risk for you to lose your home. Do you also understand that the bank will also place a lien against your house?"

"Yes, baby! Please ma'am…just give me the money. I know what I'm doing."

"How would you like your money?"

"In a cashier's check. Please make it out to Robert Stockholm dba Stockholm Financial." She passes me my cashier's check. I thank her and walk out of the bank. As I am walking to Robert's car, I notice a sly smirk on his face. "Ms. Vanetta, we *respect* your money." He reassures me that everything is going to be great and work in my favor.

"You will continue to receive the payments for your investments, but the amount will be slightly larger each time. Check your mail in a week. Now, don't tell anybody about this. It's an exclusive offer."

It seems a little odd that Robert advised me to not share our transaction with anyone, since the special investment is only for a limited amount of people. When I get home, I do what Robert told me to and don't tell anyone our secret. Surprisingly, my grandson and I get a check in the mail one week later. Robert is right, it is a bit higher than usual. Then two weeks pass by and there is nothing in the mail. I can't ask my grandson if he is still getting checks, because he will ask me about my money. My grandson has started working crazy hours and we really don't see each other that much. At that moment, I receive a text from my grandson letting me know he is going to perform next week at the nightclub he works at. The show is scheduled for seven in the evening and he wants me to put it on my calendar. Texting him back, I let him that I will be there. He also shares with me that his album and music video are complete.

Late one night, around ten, I hear Tafari on the radio, as I am browsing through the stations to find some gospel to listen to. The DJ announces Tafari, my grandson, as "one new artist to watch." That has me in tears. *My* grandson is making power moves. Listening to gospel music for over an hour, I am trying to keep the faith and wait one more week to receive another check. That would make three weeks that I haven't received anything in the mail.

The words of the personal banker are stuck in my head. If I do not pay that money back in three months, the bank can put a lien on my home and take it. I've lived in this house for over thirty years and can't see myself living anywhere else. Stress is no joke. I'm too old for this. It's clear after a month of not receiving anything that Robert has possibly scammed me. It's got me losing control of my mental faculties. It's become hard for me to remember the last time I ate a decent meal, much less taken regular showers. This worry is eating me alive. If my memory serves me right, there is a number on the bottom of the last statement that I received. Pulling myself together, I call the number. When I hear the automated message, saying, "The number you have reached has been disconnected..." I almost crap in my pants, because my worst fear has been confirmed. What am I going to do now?

At that moment, my granddaughter Nyla walks in from work. She sees me in the kitchen with my face in my hands and rushes over to me. "What's wrong grandma...You look like you just saw a ghost? Are you okay?" That's when I break down in tears. "Nyla, he took my money! He took my money!"

Nyla furrows her eyebrows curiously. "What are you talking about grandma? I don't understand. Calm down."

That's when I tell my granddaughter everything. "You did what? Gave that man twenty thousand dollars? Are you crazy grandma?"

Nyla

Immediately calling my uncle, I tell him, "Get to grandma's house ASAP."

He says, "I'm at church working on a sermon and it'll take me about thirty minutes to get there due to rush-hour traffic. "Unc, please just get here!" It only took my uncle fifteen minutes to pull up to my grandma's house. He must have drove like a bat out of hell. My grandma has a piece of paper in her hand that she is refusing to let go of.

"Grandma what is it?" I'm so scared because I've never seen her look like that.

As she faints, she drops the paper to the floor. Grabbing my phone, I dial 911, and then pick up the letter. My uncle walks through the door just in time. Giving him the 411, I watch his nostrils flare like two big tubas. "I told those fools at that bank not to give her any large amount of money without *my* authorization. I'll deal with them later!"

The ambulance arrives on time and the paramedics begin working on my grandma. My uncle and I follow the ambulance. It only takes us ten minutes to arrive, as my grandma lives very close to the hospital. Once we reach the hospital, I call Tafari and he promises to get there as soon as possible.

Tafari gets there thirty minutes later. Grandma's doctor comes out to give us her prognosis.

"Your grandmother is fine, but her heart is a little weak. She suffered a panic attack. We are going to keep her for a few days to get her blood pressure down."

My uncle speaks up and volunteers to spend the night. We discuss taking shifts to see that she is okay around the clock. That's when my uncle pulls me to the side. "Nyla, I need you to find them. With me being a pastor, that puts me at risk of losing my church. It won't look good if I don't get on this immediately though. Hunt them down and get them for what they did to your grandma. If you leave it up to me, I'll tell you to hunt them and bring them back dead, or alive." My uncle must've forgot what I do for a living.

It's not like we're back in the old cowboy days. Wanted dead or alive? That was a bit much, but they would pay for what they did to my grandma. Was I an idiot or what? I was starting to fall in love with *that* married man.

Grandma's stint in the hospital is tough on all of us. Making sure she gets her rest as well as keeping the media away is exhausting. The three of us take shifts to watch grandma. She is released after three days. Her discharge instructions are to rest and avoid major stress as much as possible. Grandma always gets the best and we pamper her as much as possible.

My uncle goes down to the bank to find out what happened and why they would allow grandma to take up to twenty stacks without calling him. He found out that her personal banker Ty was off that day. The young girl that gave grandma the cashier's check didn't read the rest of the memo's notes. My uncle puts a freeze on grandma's account. She is not allowed to take out *any* money without his authorized signature.

Once I collect my thoughts, I contact my crew and tell them about what happened. They all agree to jump on it and set up a 1-800 number for a tip line. They want me to focus solely on my grandma, while they focus on Robert and Kathy. My boss agrees to give me some time off during my grandma's hospitalization. Now that she's out of the hospital, it's time to track Robert. One of my coworkers call to inform me that they received a tip from the tip line. Someone spotted Robert and Kathy in Mexico City, Rome, Barcelona and even Bermuda. The word on the street is, if Robert and Kathy make it to Bermuda, they can disappear without a trace. These two think they are so slick. They shut down business operations and fled the country with everybody's money. My grandma and brother are near and dear to my heart. It sickens me to know that their money was stolen. The mission is to find them by any means necessary. With all my investigation skills, I find out where they're staking out. There is a picture on the wall of a model. Her name is listed as *Maddie*. This Maddie's a model/actress; not Kathy's mother. These guys are real professionals.

Robert and Kathy left a paper trail with fake stocks, dummy statements and invoices. After my co-worker and I go through all their crap, we find out that my grandma was paying my brother and my brother was paying my grandma. It was basically a pyramid scheme where each member paid each other. It was only a matter of time for this domino effect to come full circle and all come tumbling down.

As we are leaving the house Robert and Kathy were living in, Tafari calls.

"Sis, I'm playing next Friday at the club. Are you and your coworkers coming?"

Even with everything going on, I tell him, "I won't miss it for the world."

"Bring as many people as you can to the show sis."

"Of course." As important as his show is to me, I want to go into the office, because we have access to a system that can track people with their social media accounts. It is imperative that we track Robert and Kathy's online footprint to see where they are posting from. That ends up being a good decision, because Kathy's sister posted that their mother passed away. She states that the funeral is going to be the next week. I place a call to one of my coworkers and tell them we need to set a trap. It's a possibility they will return to the states for the funeral.

My coworkers let me know that I can always depend on them. Working with people like them is rare, so I am truly blessed. Deciding to stay at the office a little while longer, I get a call from my uncle. "Meet me at your grandma's house. All three of us need to talk."

Uncle LaMarcus had my brain working overtime with all types of scenarios. "What is really going on? Is everything okay? What do you need me to do?"

He assures me that all will be well when we meet. As I'm pulling up in the driveway, my uncle is pulling up behind me. Behind him is my brother. We greet one another and gave each other hugs.

We all walk in the house together. Grandma is upstairs sleeping, which is probably a good thing. All three of us sit down at the kitchen table. Uncle LaMarcus clears his throat and then starts talking. "This is the hardest thing I've ever had to say. Your grandma lost the house."

Tafari punches the wall in frustration and I bite my bottom lip. The tears feel like they are blinding me as they run down my face. "Are you serious?" I cry.

Tafari is just shaking his head no.

"Tafari, Nyla, it's true. Your grandma took out a second mortgage on the house. She only had three months to pay it back and because she does not have the money, the bank is taking the house."

That's when my brother speaks up. "Wish I had known that. I spent all my money on dropping my album next Friday. Could have helped my grandma out, but it's too late now. My money is invested too deep. I just bought a house and my album got picked up for a major label. They advanced me some money, so I can put a down payment on my house." My uncle stops us all from talking. "She will just have to move in with us."

Tafari gives our uncle a blank stare. "You know grandma don't like your wife. It's settled. My house is big enough for all three of us as it is here...I've got five bedrooms." Tafari means well, but a grown woman like me needs her space. What if I want to entertain a man? All these things I must consider.

"Thanks bro! I'll think about it." Looking at Uncle LaMarcus with my serious face, I retort, "Who's going to break the bad news to grandma?" That's when I got up because I hear her coming downstairs.

"Good night, unc. Good night, bro. I'm out. I don't want to be in the same room when you tell grandma." Tafari quickly jogs up the stairs behind me. "I'm right behind you Nyla! Unc, you on your own!"

"Why's everyone leaving the room in such a hurry?" Grandma wonders.

That's when my uncle pulls her into a tight hug. "Mother, can you sit down. We have to talk." It is quiet as a church mouse. But then, all I hear is a loud cry of agony. My brother and I can hear my grandma's sobs. We do not want to go down to see her like that. We knew she was going to be very hurt. I hear my uncle leave and my grandma closes the door to her room. For the next few days, my grandma is not talking at all.

Grandma is not eating much and at night I can hear her crying. Next week is going to be very busy. I need to hunt Robert and Kathy down like a dog looking for a bone. My body can feel the weight of the overtime hours I've been logging. At least I am not alone. My coworkers put in personal hours to aid in the manhunt too. We are right on Robert and Kathy's trail like blood hounds. It's truly unbelievable that it's after eight pm and I am still at work. My brother needs me to be refreshed and pumped for his performance tomorrow. He is a dynamic artist and performer. With everything that has happened, I need him to remain focused.

As soon as I get home, I go straight to bed. The next morning when I get up at eleven am, I notice that I do not smell anything cooking. Grandma always loves to cook. Knocking on her door, I realize she is still sleep. My grandma needs *me* to cook for her, so that's what I do. When the food is finished, I knock on her door and bring her breakfast in bed. Grandma sits up and looks at me, giving me a half smile. "What a nice thing to do baby. This makes me feel appreciated."

I don't really need the thanks. Grandma always made sure I never went hungry. "You always take care of us, grandma. I love you." We share a hug.

As I am walking out of her room, teardrops begin to fall down my cheeks. My heart aches for her. All I want to do is punch Robert and his wife in the throat before throwing them behind bars. The more and more I think about what Robert and Kathy did to grandma, the angrier I got.

To clear my mind, I put on my jogging outfit and go for a run. Running and fresh air should calm my temper down. A jog around the neighborhood park will do. Who knew that I could run ten solid miles. After breaking a much needed sweat, I head on home. When I get there, my grandma has her makeup on and is dressed up.

"Where're you going young lady?" Grandma has a way of reminding you that she is not too old, or dead. She does a little shake your shimmy dance. "Did you forget about Tafari's show? I'm ready to go."

"I have to take a shower and I'll be down shortly." It is nice to see grandma moving around and behaving like her normal self.

As I am getting out of the shower, my phone rings. It is Tafari. "Hey sis, you coming? I got you a section in VIP." I'm not able to hold back my smile. Tafari thought enough of me to get me in VIP. Now that's coming up in the world.

"Even better, bro. Grandma is coming with me."

"Yes, I can't wait to see you two."

As soon as I hang up, my phone rings again. It is one of my coworkers this time. "Nyla, we found them."

Did I hear what I think I heard? "Did you find Robert and Kathy? Where are they?" My hands are trembling in anticipation.

"They have been spotted in Vegas. Our flight leaves at zero eight hundred in the morning." Simultaneously we declare, "Let's go get them!"

We get to the club just in time to hear the announcer say that my brother is up next to perform. We are in VIP, sitting around with all these ballers and money makers. They are drinking Ace of Spade champagne, Remy Martin and King Cognac. Looks like we are surrounded by the best of the best. My brother has all these chicks in there falling at his feet and screaming his name. This nice-looking guy asks me if I'd like a glass of champagne. I thank him and only have one glass. The champagne went down so smooth. No wonder it's so expensive.

Then, my grandma asks for a little. "Let me get a sip baby girl."

Looking at her like she is crazy, I laugh. "Keep sipping on that that juice, grandma." She grabs the bottle in defiance and scowls at me. "How you gon' try to tell me what to do lil' heifer. I'm older than you."

The guy chuckles. "Let grandma a get a lil' sip."

Old or not, grandma can't handle this liquor like me. "No more for you, grandma. That's it."

My brother's performance goes on without a hitch. Everyone is grooving and moving to the beat. He steps down off the stage and all the girls are trying to grab him and rip off his clothes. Tafari's become a real sex symbol and star. As he is coming over to the VIP table, the girls start to follow him. His bodyguard has to help fight them off. When did my brother get a bodyguard? I chuckle to myself. We sit down at the VIP table and he introduces us to his promoter. It's the guy that offered me the champagne.

"Grandma, sis, this is my promoter and the man next to him is the one that's going to put my album on his record label. I'm on my way to the next level." The owner of the label is staring hard at me while talking to Tafari. He has the audacity to lick his lips with his eyes on my breasts. "We met your sister and wow...she is beautiful," he says. At that point, I start to blush a little. This man is too fine. I'd love to wrap my legs around him after getting him out of those pants. The huge bulge in his jeans is reminding me that I need to get some and soon.

It is getting late. Leaning over, I whisper to my brother. "I have an early flight. I was told Robert and Kathy were spotted in Vegas. We were advised to lay low."

Tafari's eyes brighten at the news. "I can't believe it. Justice will finally be served." Looking Tafari in the eye, I assure him that it will. "I'm positive it will bro." Someone is staked out in front of the funeral home. Kathy's mother died and we got a good tip that she will be coming to the funeral. Kathy and Robert are going to be in a disguise. My crew and I are going to go get them."

We leave the club and when I get home I hit the sack after ripping my clothes off. Making it in time for my flight, I am so glad when we land in Vegas. Calling Rent-A-Car, I inform them I need two Cadillac Escalade trucks. The four of us head to the hotel after picking up our vehicles.

On the way, I spot a hardware store. Making an abrupt stop, I rush inside. After I get a shopping cart, I grab a shovel, rope, duct tape, a gallon of water, two dark pair of sunglasses and two hats. Walking out of that hardware store with confidence, I put my hand on my gun. Robert and Kathy messed with the wrong family. Once I get back to the hotel one of my coworkers starts knocking on my door.

"We got a tip called in. Robert and Kathy showed up at the funeral," he informs me.

My blood pressure starts to boil and my heart is racing. All I want is to get revenge on them so badly. My hands are shaking as we jump in the trucks.

"I want to be the one to place handcuffs on Robert," I tell them.

We all agree that Kathy will be an easy takedown. We pull up in front of the funeral home and see all the cars lined up in front. We park about a block down and walk the rest of the way. People are leaving the church as we are standing in the side alley. We watch people slowly walk down the steps. Each of us have our walkie-talkies out. Joe notices Kathy first. She is wearing a black wig, but she's a true blonde. Robert's hair is blonde instead of his natural red. My other two coworkers go to get one of the trucks and park on the side of alley. It is just like out of a movie. We planned to do a snatch and grab. I grab Kathy and whisk her away. Joe grabs Robert and we drive about two miles before pulling over.

The team snatches Robert from the car and roughs him up. Joe yells. "Nyla, get your cuffs, so we can lock up this loser! I'm going to cuff Kathy then we'll take them to the local sheriff's office."

"Joe, put Robert in my truck. He's riding alone with me. I need to talk to him."

Joe nods and rushes off to the put Kathy in the other truck. Once we are in the truck, Robert is crying like a little bitch. "I'm so sorry for what we did to your grandma, brother and the church members."

Is this man for real? He doesn't seem remorseful to me. "What did you do with all the money?"

Robert tries to find a comfortable position against the window as he talks. "We mostly gambled, bought expensive jewelry and other high-priced things."

That's when he tries to come on to me, oozing with game that I am not trying to hear. "You know I've always liked your beautiful lips and beautiful body. If you don't turn me in, I'll take you to the money *and* rock your world. It's right here in Vegas. You can just tell your team I got away."

Calling the team, I tell them that I am stopping to get a bite to eat and will see them shortly at the station.

"Be very careful Nyla."

"Ten four," I say.

Driving to a nearby motel on the strip, I take Robert into the room, but don't remove his handcuffs.

"I'm gonna strip search you and then I'm gonna make you my bi..."

He cuts me off. "Can you unhandcuff me, so I can touch you?"

Instead of answering, I remove his clothes and then his boxers. When I look between his legs, I realize I am right. He's packing at least seven good inches and it's thick. That would be such a waste in a prison cell. Grabbing it, I jack him off until he is nice and hard. Then I grab a condom from my purse and roll it down his engorged shaft. It sounds crazy, but I'm so horny, I take advantage of the opportunity. True, I'm mad about what he did to my grandma and my brother, but I am going to release that frustration. For the moment, he's only like a sex toy to me.

"Please, can you remove the handcuffs," he asks again.

"I think it's much freakier this way..." With that said, I climb on top of him, slide down on his hardness and start grinding in circles. In no time he is moaning and groaning his pleasure. His pupils are rolling back and he's biting down on his bottom lip.

"Ohhh...damn... you feel so amazin'. I'll leave my wife for you." His eyes are bugging out and his pupils are rolling back in ecstasy.

"Shut up!" I snap before riding him faster and faster.

"Ohhh... ohh... myyy... Nyla... myyy goodness! You're gonna kill me... ahhhh... damn!" Being that he can't use his hands, he's writhing as the sensations travel over him. I'm moving on top of him like a feverish sexual frenzy has taken over my body. It's as if I'm a succubus trying to take his soul away. Bucking and thrashing as I grind up, down and around and around, I feel my own body weaken. Uh oh, the tingles start in my abdomen and traveled over my body in ripples. My body shakes and spasms.

"Mmm… ohhhh… yesssss!" My scream comes out as I throw my head back.

Using his body for my temporary pleasure, I finally release and my toes curl.

It's just what I needed, but I remember why I'm there. After getting dressed, I dress him. The cuffs are still intact.

"My body needed that Robert." My voice is sweet and shows no signs of what I plan to do.

"I'm happy to service you. Now are you going to let me go? I promise to take you to the money."

The whole time in the back of my mind, I want him to trust me and to tell me where the rest of the money really is. Suddenly he starts talking.

"We buried the money by a highway and I marked the spot with an X. Reach in my pocket and grab my wallet. There's a map inside with directions to where the money is."

Calling the guys, I tell them I'll be there in about thirty minutes. I keep checking in with them, so they won't become suspicious. Robert and I get in the truck and I speed off.

"We are only a few minutes from the spot. Slow down." Then he points and says, "Stop." Hitting the brakes, I look around, but there is nothing but desert surrounding us. He tells me to follow him.

"Give me a minute. I have to get something out of the trunk."

He starts walking and I follow. He has no idea there is a shovel behind my back. Robert gets on his knees and starts to dig with his hands. Just standing there, I watch him. My water and rope are nearby as he is busy digging. The minute I see that money, I'm going to shoot him and bury him in place of it. He pulls out a big bag of money and turns around. "See, I told you there was some money left."

Well, it's a little too late. Robert has to pay. My dear grandma and loving brother were hurt and I wasn't letting him get away with it. "Because you took life out of my grandma, I'm taking your life." I drew my weapon and shot him four times. Grabbing the rope, I tie his arms and legs up. My hands are bloody, but it doesn't stop me. Digging the hole deeper, I roll him in it. It has to be about ninety degrees and I am burning up. I have to pour some cold water over my head to cool down.

Covering Robert up with more sand, I turn around and walk back to the truck. Dragging the duffle bag that contains the money, I place it in the passenger seat. Calling Joe, I tell him that Robert escaped. Joe is shocked.

"Nyla, he escaped? How did you let that happen?"

"I let him use the restroom. I trusted him and he went out the back door."

Joe urges me to come to the sheriff's office to meet up with the rest of the crew.

"I'm on my way." That is a lie, because I plan to go back to the hotel to put the money up. Driving back to the hotel, I stuff the money underneath the bed until the next day.

Arriving at the sheriff's office, my face is obviously flustered. Joe quizzes me. "Are you okay?"

Trying to seem convincing, I rub my feet like they are killing me. "Yes, just a little tired from trying to chase Robert."

Joe encourages us to write out our individual statements. We did have Kathy, so we will receive a big check from the bounty.

One of my coworkers wants to celebrate. He jumps up on a chair and throws imaginary money around like he's making it rain.

"What goes on in Vegas, stays in Vegas!" He yells.

That's true. Robert's not going anywhere. I tell the guys to give me thirty minutes and I will meet them back at the hotel's bar.

* * *

The next morning, I immediately pack up the backpack of money and walk down the street to the bank. Telling the banker that I want to open a new account and deposit all this money, I notice her eyes get huge. The teller assumes that I won big at the tables.

When I leave the bank, I call my uncle and my grandma on three-way.

"I'm in Vegas. We captured Kathy and Robert, but sadly, Robert escaped."

Grandma can't wait to talk. "All dogs will have their day!"

Then my brother grabs the phone. "Just wanted you to know grandma had to move her stuff out of the house yesterday and a couple has already moved in."

Now, what did Tafari do with my stuff? All those years of saving. I am beginning to get mad.

"Sis, just so you can chill, I moved our stuff into the new house. You are going to love your bedroom. Your bathroom has a garden tub and your room overlooks the lake."

Letting out a major sigh of relief, I am anxious to move in.

"Unc, when you meet with the congregation, let them know that I did it. At least we got one of them. Maybe she can tell us where the money is. "

On the day Kathy is sentenced, she tells the judge where to locate some of the money. We are happy that we are able to recover some of it. My brother becomes a very successful rapper. Grandma loves her room and never wants for money again. I secretly put money in her account. Dressed incognito, I went to the bank and transferred the funds. I returned the money to my uncle's congregation in the same manner. All the members were very thankful.

The lesson here is, if you are a married man, never trust a single woman, because she might put you six feet under.

ABOUT MS KIM

Author, mother and Master Communicator, Kim McCall aka Travel was born the second eldest of four girls in St Paul, Minnesota. A witty and independent personality, Kim dreamed of being her own boss, while both working in and watching her father successfully manage the family business. Informed at 15 years of age that she was the surviving twin sister of an unnamed brother she began journaling to express the loss of the brother she longed to know. In 2017 she finally found her long lost siblings that she'd been searching for thirty seven years. After reflecting on the joyous and turbulent moments in her life...through hundreds of pages of life experiences, Kim felt the need to rest her pen at 18.

The birth of her daughter at age 20, ignited a fervor to write again. Kim hoped that one day her daughter would read her journals. Her two children now follow in her passion for writing and management; Kim's daughter had a story published in the Minneapolis Spokesman at the age of 12 and today manages a store for one of the world's largest grossed retail stores. She's also an aspiring model. Kim's son is an entrepreneur who owns www.gametimeacademy.org. He expresses his joy for writing through rapping and producing music. Kim was married for 12 years and is now divorced. She now knows that she is a better person in spite of the outcome. Kim currently resides in Atlanta, Georgia. She feels so free when she's writing so ladies (and gentlemen) let's get this party started!